CW01483571

Grailwriters Anthology

Gene Genii

A Grailwriter's Anthology plus guest writers

Compiled by Sharon Birch
Edited by John Riddle
Cormorant Publishing Hartlepool

Gene Genii

An Grailwriters Anthology.

Authors: Various
Published in Great Britain by Cormorant Publishing
Hartlepool

First published in 2008 by Cormorant Publishing
Hartlepool.
cormorantpublishing@yahoo.co.uk

www.riddlewrites.co.uk

ISBN 978-0-9558593-9-7
Illustrated and designed by Cormorant Publishing
Hartlepool
Compiled by John Riddle

Typeset, printed and bound by Connoisseur Crafts
Limited
Hartlepool Enterprise Centre,
Brougham Terrace,
Hartlepool. TS24 8EY
United Kingdom
email:concrafts@surfree.co.uk

Warning this book contains "adult language"

Authors

The online writer's group 'The Grailwriters' commit to a sponsored writing marathon every year.

On 6th October 2006 they raised £585.00 in sponsorship money for Jeans for Gene's day. I dare say, they even wore jeans! The money raised went to the Ehlers-Danlos Support Group as one of the Grailwriting families suffers with this condition.

A number of writers sat down for twelve hours to write as many short stories and poems as they could, based on prompt titles provided to them at the start of the event. (Hence the same titles for some stories in this book!)

The writers, from all over the UK (and one from Denmark) aged from 9 years old to ooh- about that! produced over three hundred tales between them.

This book has been a long time in the making, but thanks to Cormorant Publishing Hartlepool, the Grailwriters have been able to produce this collection of stories and poems they toiled over.

Included are some other writers linked to Grailwriters, specially invited for their variety and expertise. If you like what you read, many authors have included their own websites and details of their individual publications. We are an eclectic mix of talent!

Thank you for your support and we hope you enjoy the read!

All in the Mind or all in the Genes?

"Pull yourself together!"
That's what the Doctors say.
Easy words, yet hard to do
When your knees are giving way!
This pain of mine can not be seen
But I assure you that it's real.
You can't imagine what it's like
You don't know how I feel.
My ankles often dislocate
My thumbs bend backwards too.
My elbows crack, my hips sublux
What is a girl to do?
The muscles in my eyes are weak
Which makes me see things double.
My pelvic floor has fallen down
(That really does cause trouble).
Each day I take an afternoon nap
As my body needs to rest.
I do my physio, pop my pills
It all seems such a test!
Some say that "it's all in the mind"
But Ehlers-Danlos means
It's not in the imagination
But written in the Genes!

Sue Newson

About Genetics

Did you know...

in the UK, one baby in every 33 is born with a genetic disorder or birth defect – that's one born every 30 minutes whose life could be affected?
There are over 4,000 recognised genetic disorders, such as cystic fibrosis and 'baby in the bubble' syndrome?
Much more pioneering research is needed and that costs millions of pounds?
Genetic diseases range widely in severity. Some have very little impact on the affected person's life, while others are devastating and can lead to severe disability and even death in childhood. The only existing long term treatment for some forms of the more severe disorders is a bone marrow transplant (BMT). This is a highly risky procedure and is dependent on finding a suitable bone marrow donor and the child being well enough to undergo chemotherapy. For the majority of children with disorders which can be treated with a BMT, actually undergoing this procedure is not possible.
New therapies, such as gene therapy, are currently being developed and have the potential to revolutionise the way genetic disorders are treated. It does not rely on finding a donor and recent breakthroughs are giving many families enormous hope that a cure for their child's disorders is not too far away.
Your support of Jeans for Genes will help to speed up the development of these pioneering new therapies.

www.jeansforgenes.com

Jeans for Genes

Our mission and values

Our mission

We put our hearts and energy into raising money that:

- Provides **care** for children and families who are affected by genetic disorders

Funds ongoing research into the **causes** and **cures** for these disorders

In all that we do, we aim to raise awareness and promote understanding of genetics and what it means to be affected by a genetic disorder.

Our values

We promote understanding and tolerance through education

Genetic disorders only affect one in 33 children born in the UK, but genes affect us all. We work to increase awareness and understanding of the differences our genes create.

We put the 'human' into human genetics

Genetics is a young but increasingly significant area of science. But it's also one that can be frightening and misunderstood. Our aim is to make genes and genetics accessible, relevant and not intimidating.

We go out of our way to value and recognise everyone involved with us

We aim that everyone who makes a contribution to Jeans for Genes feels valued, appreciated and recognised. As a small charity we aim to make your relationship with us a personal one.

We are professional and transparent

We want everyone who makes a donation to Jeans for Genes or gives us their time or service, to be reassured that we are a professional and efficient organisation.

We will show you how and where we spend the money we raise and answer y our questions about Jeans for Genes as fully and as quickly as we can.

We are serious about fun!

We know that the fun of Jeans for Genes Day is one of the reasons you support us. But we never lose sight of the very real reason that the charity exists. We aim to strike a balance between the two.

Chapter 1 .. Sharon Birch

Is She Dead?

She leant back on the comfortable leather office chair. She needed to work out this plot. It was bugging her. She closed her eyes and feigned sleep. It was good to sit in the dark and quiet and reflect.

They wanted something. They always wanted something. Whispering could be heard in the kitchen. Pitter-patter on the laminate hall flooring told her they were coming

Still she sat there.

The door creaked open.

"You go."

"No! You go!"

The two sisters fought over who would ask Mummy for some juice. The eldest stepped forward in trepidation. It was dark and spooky in Mummy's office when the light was off. The books threw shadows all around the room. It was the most comfortable place in world when they curled up on her knee in her chair, but when it was like this, they were scared.

"Mummy?" whispered Giselle.

There was no answer.

"Mummy?" She tried again.

Felicity clung to her sister's arm. Both in nightdresses, they felt cold. They wished Daddy was here. They hated it when he was away on business.

"Mummy?" Giselle sounded worried, anxiety in her voice.

"Is she dead?" asked the youngest.

Just as Giselle reached out to touch the body in the chair, "BOO," shouted Mummy.

The Allotment

They arrived on the Friday and were still there on the Sunday. Ted chewed his fingernails to the quick. His eyes were wide and he played at being compliant. Inside, his guts were bubbling.

As a founder of a local campaign group for underprivileged children, he was an upright, upstanding member of the community. People looked up to him. Twenty years working in a Citizens Advice Centre helped.

He had suspected they were coming. He wasn't well heeled for nothing. Chief Inspector Bartlett had given him the nod, so he was prepared. When the team arrived, Ted was already tending to his compost heap. A fresh delivery of manure was arriving later that day.

Every night and all weekend, Ted went to his allotment. It was his safe haven from the horrors of his past, he told people. There was no-one to bother him. A widower for ten years, he kept himself busy working the earth and pottering in his shed. He loved the kids coming to help. He kept them amused for hours.

Ted didn't like mess. He liked things neat and tidy. He wanted to be ready for their arrival, so he'd painted the inside of his shed white on the Thursday night. He lit a fire and watched it lick and destroy the rubbish lying about that he'd piled up - the rubbish, the porn, the kids' toys, the soiled panties and everything else that might incriminate him.

It was an ingenious idea of his - moving the compost from the back of the shed to the side of the allotment to bury the laptop deep underground. Piling the compost high above it made sure that piece of evidence was buried.

Nightmares of the past flickered in and out of his head as Ted watched the policemen trash his haven without compassion. Recalling his boyhood, being abused by the calloused hands of Uncle Ted in the very same allotment, he wished they'd come when he was boy. It might have saved him – and those victims of his own.

Expect the Worst

They told me to hold his hand and talk to him. The doctor explained that we should expect the worst.

The worst? What was that? What *exactly* did it mean? And to whom did it relate?
I could not feel sad, and I will not cry in sorrow if he dies today. We, his family, will rejoice.

Callous? No.   Human? Yes. We didn't live his life. They didn't live ours. Only others in our situation can understand.

At fifteen, Samuel was nearly a man. It is obscene to watch him struggle as he becomes older. As a child, it was easier. Now, he is more cumbersome than ever. It is impossible to lift him. At fifteen he has hormones raging through his impotent body and the anger behind his eyes shines through. It is difficult to control him and to watch his confusion and his misery. Tempers rain in his head. We know, we can tell by the way he expresses himself with motion and with noise.

If Samuel was a pet, we would have done the honourable thing a long time ago. He isn't, he is our son. I love him, his father loves and his sisters love him. It is increasingly difficult to live with him, for him to be with us.

The time is coming when he will have to leave but I don't want it to be to residential care.

When he contracted pneumonia from simply inhaling his vomit one morning when the rest of us were sleeping, we had to let the hospital take over. They told us he was in the best place. I would rather he was at home with us.

Now, as we sit by his bedside and his organs fail, the medical staff fuss about, trying to make him comfortable. He has never been comfortable. His eyes have told me, even when we made him laugh.

When he passes, and it will be soon, it won't be the worst that could happen. We have given everything we could to our beautiful son with cerebral palsy. For someone with his disabilities we have ensured he has had the best quality of life that he could.

Go away and hate us. We know what the worst is. He has lived it.

Elegant in Black

I dressed for the occasion. It was meant to be a fitting tribute to the man I'd once adored. He would appreciate the gesture, I'm sure. I have no idea how long he had worked on the idea.

A while I would guess.

Things hadn't been running smoothly for about two years. We argued and when we stopped arguing, we were silent. We started to live separate lives. Once we had been so much together. Now we lived like strangers. The absence of children saw our differences emerge. He did his thing and I did mine. We began to like it like that.

With two different lifestyles to behold, we spent two lots of income. We had a generous income and had great spending power, but instead of enjoying the same hobbies, we took diverse paths. The cost of separate routines increased our outgoings until we found ourselves financially strapped.

A decade older than I, Peter wanted the finer things in life whereas I wanted more exciting pastimes. He took up writing and shooting. I chose canoeing and adventure holidays. Therefore, it was a surprise for me to find his sudden interest in water sports.

He hadn't returned home one evening but I had become used to that. I didn't always make it home myself, so I could hardly complain. It was just unusual. The next morning, I found the letter. I checked and my canoe was missing. He had taken it out for a sojourn. I was to call the police and report him missing if he didn't arrive back.

I duly did as he asked. I also became worried. I was really rather fond of the old goat.

Three days later, my canoe was washed ashore, broken, battered and forlorn. Parts of his clothing were found with it. No body.

His four wheel drive stood untouched on our gravel drive. His personal items stood in my bathroom. His side of the bed was untouched.

I pillaged the computer looking for clues. I found them. A secret bank account and a mistress in America led me to a hidden web page. He had created it for me. I guess he must have known I'd go looking. He loved me as a brother, cared for me deeply but our lives had dispersed and it was now time to go our own ways forever. The life insurance would see me right. He had other money put aside for his own needs. I just had to see it out and not bottle it. The loss would be all mine.

As I stand here, in front of the crowd, a memorial for him now he is legally declared dead, I am elegant in black, the grieving widow.

Orange Colour

There are things that a woman just knows. She sees the tell tale signs and it's simple. It stares right back at her. How does one deal with it? Maureen struggled to understand.

Almost every night for months she had gone to bed

before he was home. She had lain awake until she heard the turn of the lock and listened as he tried to be quiet. Once he was in the house, she allowed a sigh of relief and it was only then she could sleep.

It was starting to affect her work. She was constantly tired. Doris at the next desk had been through it but Sarah was newlywed and had it all to come. She didn't envy her.

His mobile phone was constantly ringing and one night he'd left it behind on the kitchen windowsill. She ignored it. After an hour, he flew in the house and snatched it up, pleased to see it in the place where he'd left it. He looked at her accusingly but she had been strong. She hadn't looked.

Maureen pondered over the last twenty years. He had relied on her so much in the early days. They had been close. He told her everything; what bothered him, how sad or how happy he was. Now it was just the two of them left rattling around in the house, she feared everything between them had gone.

He was working now and found employment where many others couldn't. There was surplus cash for his pleasures. Maureen prayed he hadn't got himself involved in gambling or some other addictive pastime. His mates had ceased to pop around so it could only be a woman. She hoped he had found himself nice lass. Not a slapper or that sort. It really would be a punch in the solar plexus.

Last week he had challenged Maureen. He told her that they needed to talk. She agreed to give him some space. In the heart, she knew it was the right thing to do. She had to let go if she wanted to salvage anything.

Yesterday, she saw confirmation as he came downstairs after his shower. His legs were a bright orange colour. Maureen couldn't help it as she laughed. He was offended. What was wrong with going on the sunbed? She laughed some more. Sunbed? Six minutes! It broke the tense situation and made her see it as it really was, placing things in perspective.

She told him, "Son, you have your own life. Get on with it."

Sharon Birch is a writer, originally from the North East of England but now living in the Scottish Highlands. With success in flash fiction and short story markets, she has been published in a variety of magazines and ezines. Sharon is currently writing 'Living  with Fred,' a factual book about Ehlers-Danlos Syndrome, a genetic condition that affects her and her three children. It is to be published early 2009. Her novel will soon follow.

Living with FrED

By SHARON BIRCH

One family's perspective on living in the shadow of the heriditable genetic condition known as Ehlers-Danlos Syndrome (type III -Hypermobility)

An informative, knowledgeable view of the effects of EDS, relevant to all affected by this often disabling condition – families, medics and professionals alike. It is told with practicality and the unassuming humour of a mother, wife and fellow sufferer.

To order this book:
Email: **shazzabirch@aol.com**
By post to: **13 The Green,
Seaton Carew, Hartlepool,
TS25 1AS**

The book is priced at £7.99 plus £2 postage and is produced by
Cormorant Publishing Hartlepool
www.riddlewrites.co.uk

Chapter 2 …. Steve Birch

Showdown at the Hoedown

The scene was set. A country band were playing, cowboys and their girls were dancing and whooping.

The door flew open and the rest of the bar turned to look. The musicians stuttered in their playing before grinding to a halt, drinks stopped twixt cup and lip. No-one knew what to do or say.

Kincaid ambled to the bar, drunk and surly but full of pain.

He stood at the bar and the tender gave him his usual whiskey before scuttling away, embarrassed.

"Make me laugh before I kill some poor fucker. I've had enough."

No-one spoke, not even his friends. They were frightened too. Maybe it was too late.

"*Make me laugh before I kill some poor fucker. I've had enough.*" Louder, sadder. The same reaction.

None

Kincaid stood up, 5' '7". Drunk and angry, now 7' 3". He screamed and took his pistol out. People backed off.

He laid it on the bar and burst into tears.

"For Christ's sake, this is Hull, not the real West. I've been coming to this stupid club for seven years. You could speak to me before my wife died of cancer, why not now? It's been a fortnight, everyone's disappeared."

He pulled out another gun, smaller, less showy but obviously *real.*

There was a noise, and Kincaid (Barry Smith) went down as bits of his head slid down people's faces and various bar furnishings.

In full club costume, he died. With his boots on.

Bar None

Picture this. A bar full of men, many of them are a bit drunk, some are on their way, some just starting. All are well and *tastefully* dressed, clean and if scented, then nicely. Not a football shirt or badly fitting item of sports clothing in sight. Not that many beer bellies either. No farts. Proper conversation, relaxed and apparently informed.

The toilets are clean and well appointed.

Barbra Streisand is singing her little heart out through speakers that not only sound good but match the décor perfectly.

Two such men have just renewed an acquaintance at the bar.

"Hello Barry – God, what happened to your face? I haven't seen a black eye like that in years…"

"I was in a gay bar last night and spoke to a really nice-looking guy who was softly-spoken and friendly. When I tried to move things on a bit he hit me really hard. Turns out he was a marine who was happy to sit round and have his beer bought by gays that wanted to be seen with him."

"So when he hit you, did his hand move from left to right, or right to left?"

"For Christ's sake, from right to left – I think. What the bloody hell difference does *that* make?"

"Aaaah… Anti-clockwise…"

Caramel Coloured Leaves

A certain weather presenter once said that there nothing to worry about, certainly no hurricane.

One of my best friends worked for the local council, the

grandly named 'London Borough of Tower Hamlets', so named because it contained the Tower of London.

It would be a bit like calling my wife Fort Knox because she has a gold tooth.

As we know, the hurricane struck. My friend was a tree surgeon by title, but at 19 or 20 he would readily admit that the title was grander than the job, and that he was more like a skilled pruner. Maybe they all are.

My memory is good but only as good as I think – or remember – it is.

I remember the devastation, trees on cars, trees on houses, trees on the ground, trees on trees on the ground. Caramel coloured leaves, stripped slightly prematurely from their bases. Everywhere you looked. Perversely, it was quite nice. The leaves filled the places that would usually be occupied by McDonald cartons. A bit like the way a fall of snow can make the shittiest part of wherever you live look beautiful for a sadly short time.

If I were Doctor Who, I would go back and kill Mr. McDonald, certainly the man that invented polystyrene cartons, the man that invented stone cladding and anyone that thought of time-share. Sod history and ripples through vortexes.

Perhaps the industrial Japanese would celebrate those few short days of snow over dirt as they celebrate their blossoms, appreciating the beauty and brevity in a way that we can't. I think we could if we had the courage to even approach mortality.

Anyhow.

I was much older than my friend, big lad, a bit thick but I knew his parents. I remembered him as little. I loved him. I had been a bit of a mate, a bit of a brother and a bit of a Dad. I had told him off about doing speed both in his car and up his nose. I had confiscated his butterfly knife – for the uninitiated, a horrid, lethal weapon – that he started to carry because he 'wanted to protect himself.'

We nearly came to blows over that.

Anyway, the only time I ever saw him cry was when I went with him to the local park and he saw his trees. Cry he did and no mistake. Those trees had had more love from him than he had ever received or had the time to give.

He pointed to a special type of Lime tree – lost on me – and said, "It's the only one in London. It was mine. Where are we going?"

I just said "From here." And I gave the big strong thug a cuddle as he wept and wept and wept.

Steve Birch is the husband of Sharon. He recently celebrated the thirtieth anniversary of his twenty first birthday. That should tell you all you need to know. He says.

Chapter 3 …. Matthew Birch (age 9)

Graveyard High (Prompt – Old School House)

Nobody liked Necropolis high school the teachers are just so deathly strange. The year is 2121 and not one of the kids who go to Necropolis high trusts the teachers. Why the teachers are so eager to get out of a hot place, never mind that, even in a warm place they want to get out.

Not even one student knew what necropolis meant, yet…

Attached to the school was an old infant school and near that was a 1527 year old graveyard and as people said you go into those places you never go out! Only bad kids, (no really bad kids) go in there as people leave as dusty skeletons, though very rarely they found a body and even if they did it would be in a hole as if trying to get them back, for something. Larry said to his friend" I sure wouldn't want to go to bad or I'll march with the infantry" Lewis, (his friend) laughed. So did you here we've got a trip to, he stopped," no trip for you two, the only place you're going is the old infant school" Lewis screamed," what for?

The teacher said," Talking in class, off you go".

It had been several months since they had seen Larry and Lewis, now pets were going missing rapidly. It was mainly fierce dogs and a few wolves are coming and disappearing. The teachers seem to know a lot about the subject. The teachers are saying that Larry and Lewis are on holiday but for four month's? Seriously I'm trying to convince my parents to let me go to Pitts Landing High School though I'm begging them to let me. Naturally they're as weird as my teachers.

Matthew Birch is 11yrs old and he loves to write sci-fi stories, chapters and chapters of them. He enjoys Darren Shan books and there is nothing he can't tell you about Harry Potter. He has ruled out wanting to be astronaut in favour of one day making his living writing fantastic books.

Chapter 4 …. Elizabeth Birch (age 10)

A Tidey End (aka A deal's a deal)

Imogen Nogspotter was a very cheeky, daring twelve-year-old girl, who went to a boarding school by the sea.

One day, when she went to a normal school, she came home with bright green hair. Her parents had said, "What's happened this time?" and she had replied, "Andrew called me stupid so I said at least I'm more daring than you and he dared me to dye my hair green so I did." So her parents said... "Right, we've had enough. You're going to a boarding school, we've already arranged it. You were going to go next year, but we can rearrange that!" So she started Miss Wooding-Spike's boarding school for girls the week after.

Imogen had a friend at her boarding school called Francis, but her nickname was Frankie. One thing about Frankie was that she sometimes just went off with this other girl, Alice, and Imogen hated that because Frankie was the only reason she stayed there. If she hadn't made friends with Frankie, then she would have run away long ago. The dinners tasted like sick, the lessons were hard, the homework was the most boring thing ever, Miss Wooding-Spike was always mean to her and she was always picked last for sports. But Frankie made her feel better. They had so much fun that it didn't matter about the other things. Except Alice.

Alice was mean to everybody but Frankie. Everyone liked Frankie, but she only wanted to be friends with Imogen. And Alice.

One day, Alice was laughing at Imogen because the night before, she had sneaked into her dormitory and put blue hair dye into her shampoo. Imogen turned up at maths late with blue hair.

"Imogen Nogspotter, what have you done to yourself?" asked the maths teacher, half angry, half concerned.

"It's not my fault, Miss. Someone put something in my shampoo, Miss. And I think I know exactly who," said Imogen angrily, glaring at Alice.

"Well I don't tolerate tale-telling, so please take your seat and find out what we have been doing for the last ten minutes." said the maths teacher.

Imogen was grumpy to find out that they had been doing fractions. At break time, she walked around, talking to Frankie.

"That Alice! She's so horrible. I don't see why you like her, Frankie. She should be expelled." moaned Imogen.

"Why should she? It was just a harmless prank. I don't see why you hate her!" Said Frankie. "You're the one who should be expelled, you've been late to every maths lesson this week. And English and History and Geography!"

"Fine, if you don't want me as your friend anymore, I'll leave!" Said Imogen.

"Fine! See if I care!" shouted Frankie.

So that night, Imogen waited until her room-mates were fast asleep and packed her things. She left her room, and went to the toilet one last time. She realised that she would have to either swim or walk for miles along the beach until she reached her little village.

She decided to walk, she wasn't all that great at swimming and it would be very cold in the sea.

She sneaked down to the kitchen and made lots of sandwiches, using a whole loaf of bread. She put them in a bag and tied the top up.

She crept out of the school, and walked onto the beach. The tide started coming in! The sea was very deep, she'd had swimming lessons in it before. This is the end, she thought. She saw someone emerge from the fog and grab her. The next thing she knew, she was sitting in a blanket on the wall in front of the sea with Frankie.

"Frankie! I thought you didn't care about me anymore!" said Imogen.

"Yeah, well... Alice started talking about you, saying you're so stupid that you probably have to get someone to do your laces for you on a morning, and I said that she's the stupid one because I can't do my laces either and you can, and she just stormed off and said she doesn't know why she ever liked me." Frankie said.

"Frankie! I can't believe she said that! Well, I can really, because she's that sort of person, but how mean of her! So are we friends again?" Imogen said.

"Best friends forever!" Frankie said. "As long as you never run away again – or at least try to – because you're very heavy to carry on to a wall!"

"Deal!" laughed Imogen.

So the two friends walked back into the school, and crept back up to their dormitories.

I found it under the table

You wouldn't believe the things my brother and sister drop under the table!

I'm Mary. My brother's Joseph, my sister's Eve. My mum wanted us to have nice, respectable names.

As I was saying, you wouldn't believe the things my siblings drop under the table! And it gets left there, too.

One day, I was searching for my cat-shaped earrings. Neither my brother or sister have their ears pierced, so they couldn't have taken them.

I started looking under the table, and I found this weird fluffy thing. I sighed, and blew it away. It sort of turned around (all by itself!) and got bigger. It uncurled itself to reveal... a face!

It started rolling around, sucking everything up - including my cat earrings! - and it suddenly flew out of the window.

Everyone was screaming and going wild over the big fluffball thing. It got bigger the more it sucked in. Everyone saw my guilty face, and yelled "Where did it come from!?" And I replied, "I found it under the table."

Elizabeth Birch will be 13 when this book is published. She enjoys reading, writing, and all kinds of drama.
Her favourite authors are Jacqueline Wilson, JK Rowling and Roald Dahl. She hopes to 'become famous – darling!'

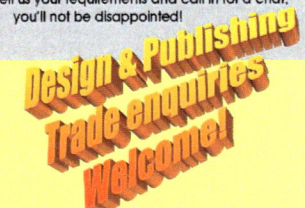

Chapter 5 … Lewis Humphries

To Do List

"Will you mow that bloody lawn, Lewis?" Her voiced raged from the distance of the kitchen, almost inaudible above the streaming taps and churning tumble dryer.

I sighed, slowly leaning forward and placing my half-drunk tea cup upon the table. Reaching to the right, I pulled my 'to do' list from an overgrown pile of loose paper beside the settee, and a dark inked ball point pen that nestled at the summit. With the document in my hand, I scrolled through to page 117, and scribbled a joined up note on the leaf. "Must mow lawn," it read, its letters placed messily beneath the previous entries.

Through to the living room from the kitchen, she strode towards me purposefully. "What on earth is the point of that list, Lew? If that even qualifies as a list now. There are less pp in the bible."

I paused looked up at her. "The point, my dear, is simply to prioritise things. So now, when I start, I have a clear path to follow, and a sequence that I can adhere to." A knowing grin lit my face, as I met the darkness of her stare.

"Start? When exactly are you going to start?"

"Well sweetness," I said, handing her the pp, "take a look at number 1."

She took the paper in her hands and looked searchingly for point number 1. Her eyes found a clear, large lettered scribe at the head of the piece.

"Read it," I said, noting the confused expression that contorted her face.

She cleared her throat and turned her glance to the page. "Point number one - Achieve inner fulfilment and happiness."

After a moments silence, she meet his gaze. "So you see honey, it's one thing at a time. It has to be."

My Wanted Husband

All the women want my husband.

I see them, their envious eyes seeking him out as he moves, admiring the smooth handsomeness of his visage. They whisper amongst themselves, allowing brief, hushed giggles of laughter to pass their shadowed lips.

So too, they notice the neat cut of his dark grey suit, fitted aptly to his broad frame. Their faces flicker gently, realising that a man who has a suit like that must have money and prospects, the rewards of a high powered job in the city. Then, as he walks towards me he smiles a warm, handsome smile, its glow lingering between the firmness of his cheekbones. A pause, followed by a sweet, tender kiss that meets my waiting lips and melts into memory and beyond. As he peels away, I note the admiring looks his way, and the obvious flames of jealousy that flicker towards me. If only they knew, as I did, that packaging can be deceiving.

As I turn to pour another drink, the wording of a question filters through my mind, and rests upon the rear of my tongue. 'If all these women want my husband so much, why don't they just take him?'

One child too many

As I sup the dregs from the drained whisky tumbler in my hand, I watch her cradle our son in her arms. She is sweet and attentive, nurturing him into a soft, lulling sleep. I tilt my head gently as he drifts into unconsciousness, her slender fingers tickling the faint blond of his hair. Her eyes are fixed on our boy, so much so that she doesn't me milling in the bedroom doorway, nor even motions as I edge quietly from the landing and down the staircase.

Turning back into my living room, I head towards the table and pour another scotch. The dark liquor flows into the waiting crystal, its scent inflaming the need of my hunger. I hear her footfall above, as she leaves our son's bedroom and heads across the landing to our own, pulling the door to rest as she does so. Taking a sip of my drink, I prick my ears as she clambers onto the mattress, and I imagine her pulling the covers up close around her neck for warmth. Within seconds she will be asleep, cast free in her dreams and without care whilst I stare into the wide-eyed gaze of insomnia.

I cannot help but think of that sweet embrace and silk like touch, and I cannot help but remember when she was mine. You see, we may only have one child, but is one too man.

She never saw it coming.

She was blinded by her love and devotion, bound by the weight of her feelings. No force of nature could cast those shackled chains, nor could the relentless march of time sway her path. And no matter how the words were spoken, they were impossible to comprehend.

"Darling, I'm leaving you."

Sugary Love (for Karen and Laura)

Alone at last - spare for Karen, Laura and their darling. All the stresses and the anguish of life are slumbering in the darkness, forgotten for a few hours of sacred twilight. Children and men are asleep, their plentiful needs without care for the time being, and not even the low hum of television can draw their attention to what is to come

Laura, basking the silence of the hour, reaches deep into her handbag and fumbles for a moment. Then, her searching hand finds the treasure she is wanting. 'Ah, there you are,' she whispers, gently pulling her hand from the bag.

There, resplendent in the bright lamplight, is 6 inches of pure bliss. A dark, cocoa brown sheath is wrapped tight around its form, compressing the sweet, rich heaven that lies beneath it. Tentatively, Laura unwraps the object and there, in all its light-brown glory, is a tapered slice of milk chocolate, slightly melted in the searing heat of the summer month.

"Ah, sugary love," says Laura, handing a fragmented piece to Karen. "God bless you."

Lewis Humphries is 26 and currently lives in Birmingham, England with his wife. He writes in his spare time with an ambition to make it into a career, focusing mainly on poetry and short fiction of anything between 500 and 3000 words.

Chapter 6 … Claire Nixon

No need to panic

"Dave," Susan shouted, from upstairs. Dave took a swig of lager and turned the TV up. "Go on there," he cheered as the footballers on screen played.

"Dave," this time she shouted a little but louder.

"For goodness sake woman, shut up." Again, he turned the TV up more. Perched on the edge of his seat he cheered for his team

"DAVE!"

He fell off the edge of his seat, spilling his lager all over himself. "Wow woman, do you have to creep up behind me and shout."

Susan held onto the back of the sofa, her knuckles turning white. "Dave," she said, through gritted teeth.

"What man? I'm trying to watch the match."

"Stuff the match, it's time."

"No it ain't, ain't time for another ten minutes, love."

He stood up and looked at the TV. "Go on there, son."

"You b...... imbecile, I'm not talking about that." She rubbed her large stomach. "I think I'm in labour."

His eyes widened. "You're joking, couldn't you wait till the match was finished?"

Susan bent forward, squeezing the back of the sofa again, her teeth ground as she breathed through flared nostrils. Sweat formed on her brow.

"Oh, man. You look like the Hulk when you do that. S...! You're in labour."

"I know I'm in labour – get me to the blooming hospital now!

Dave ran from one side of the living room to the other

flinging his arms in circles, saying to himself, "No need to panic. No need to panic. We've practised this many times. Oh, man." He stopped in front of Susan. "What do I do?"

Susan grabbed his arm, squeezed and screamed, "I think the baby is coming now."

Dave gulped. His eyes rolled into the back of his head. Then he collapsed on the floor.

"I knew it," Susan said, she stepped over him and opened the front door. "Mum, you can come in now."

Dave's' mother walked in and shook her head, opened her purse and gave her a hundred pounds. "You win."

"Thanks Jean, told you I'd be able to drag him away from the match near the end."

"When he wakes he'll be expecting to see the baby."

"Don't worry, I'll just tell him it was a false alarm, this little tyke is staying where he is for at least another four weeks."

They walked into the kitchen, stepping over Dave.

"It's Halloween soon," Jean said, "we'll have to think of something to do to him then."

`"Have I ever told you you're the world's best mother-in-law?"

Doomed cargo

"Sir, may I ask permission for you to pass this task to someone else."

"So, you've heard."

"Yes, sir."

"And what is it you've heard?"

"Well, sir, I've heard that those who have touched that crate have died under unusual circumstances and within twenty-four hours. It's doomed cargo, sir."

"So, you're saying the cargo is cursed."

He looked at the wooden crate and gulped. "Yes, sir.

"I don't believe in that type of nonsense."

"Sir, permission to speak freely." Beads of sweat formed on his brow.

"Permission granted."

"If you don't believe in that type of nonsense, sir, then you can move it, sir." He nervously looked back at the crate.

"I would, but I am not paid for that type of work."

"Sir, please, I beg you, pass the task onto someone else. I have children, they need me."

"And who should I pass this task onto? That is, if I relieved you of your duties."

"Reynolds, sir."

"And why should I do this?"

"He's been seeing your wife for the past month, sir."

"And what proof do you have of this?" His nostrils flared as he tried to keep a straight face.

"Here sir, I have video footage on my phone." He rummaged in his pocket, took out the phone, selected the video and passed it to him.

"I'll be keeping a hold of this for the time being."

"Yes, sir."

"Dismissed." He spun around and stormed to the other side of the warehouse. "Reynolds, you're to take this crate to 'C' block -- alone."

The Allotment

"What lovely cabbages you have," Mr Thomson said, admiring the vegetables in the allotment. He looked over to the other vegetable patches; none of them grew vegetables the way Mr Greene did. All of Greene's vegetables had vibrant colours and all were twice the size of the other vegetables grown in the allotment. "I'd love to know your secret."

Mr Greene put down his garden fork and smiled. "I'm glad you asked. My secret ingredient is in the shed."

Thomson followed Greene inside of his metal shed.

"Do you have a light in here. I can't see a thing."

"Here, hold my hand, sit here." Thomson followed his directions and sat down.

"What's that smell?"

"The fertiliser."

"It has an unusual aroma… what the?" Thomson's arms were clamped down to the chair, then a lamp was turned on.

"What on earth do you think you're doing?"

"Showing you how I make my fertiliser." He placed a piece of duct tape across his mouth and made sure his arms were secure then he placed a syringe in his vein. "It's pretty simple really." The tube from the syringe went inside of a small metal box. "This is the pump." From the metal box, another tube headed to a barrel. "And this is where I store the fertiliser."

Thomson's eyes widen as he watched his blood being pumped into the metal box and out into the barrel.

"Don't worry Mr Thomson, I'll make sure your carcass doesn't go to waste – my wife will be so pleased to make pies out of you. You know that gravel path I'm making that you're so amazed with, well, your bones will be ground down and added to that – you see, I don't use real gravel."

eBay

"Oh I like this," Mavis said, inspecting the fine detailed ornament.

"I bought it from eBay, only paid a few quid for it," Jan replied.

Mavis smiled and put the ornament down. "Oh, now I do like this mirror of yours, it's like the one I used to have, one of the children broke it. Cost me a small fortune."

"I bought it from eBay, only paid a few quid for it," Jan replied.

"I love the way you've decorated, it's so bright and cheery. The curtains are divine."

"I bought them from eBay, only paid a few quid for them."Jan replied.

They walked out of the living room into the kitchen. Mavis admired the willow-patterned crockery. "These are supposed to be worth a fair amount these days."

"I bought them from eBay, only paid a few quid for them," Jan replied.

They walked out of the backdoor into the garden. "Now this is very nice." She looked at a young man, sipping lemonade, on a nearby deckchair, wearing a small tight pair of trunks. "Log me on your computer Jan, I want one of those too."

Eyes at the Back of My Head

"Put that down," I say, as I wash the dishes.

Charlie puts the cookie jar down and slowly starts to pry the lid off the biscuits.

"You can put that down too."

"How do you know what I'm doing?"

"I've got eyes at the back of my head."

"Very funny, mum." He sticks his tongue out."

"I'll cut that off one of these days."Charlie frowns and holds up his middle finger.

"Do you want me to break that too?"

"I didn't do anything."I pull the plug out of the sink and dry my hands. "I told you, I've got eyes at the back of my head, I see everything."

Charlie sticks his tongue out and runs out of the kitchen. I close the door behind him and part the hair on the back of my head, then I take out the eye drops from pockets. Tilting my head forwards, I drop a single droplet into each eye on the back of my head; sometimes my hair irritates my eyes.

The kitchen door swings open, I jump and drop the eye drops on the floor.

"What you doing?" Charlie asks, picking up the bottle of drops. "Just putting some eye drops in the eyes at the back of my head."

"Mum, I'm seven now, don't you think I'm a bit old for that silly story?"

Broken Bodies

They lie at the bottom of the cliff. Their broken bodies bent over the rocks, waiting for the tide to come in, to take them out to sea.

At the top of the cliff, a little blonde girl holds onto her dolly, weeping. A curious couple approaches her.

"Are you okay little one?" The elderly woman asks.

The little girl shakes her head.

"What's wrong poppet?" The elderly man says, wiping her tears on his handkerchief.

"It's my mummy and daddy, they've… they've."

"They've what? Left you here alone?"

She shook her head and pointed to the edge of the cliff. "They fell."

The elderly couple gasped, and headed to look over the edge. The little girl ran after them and pushed them over the edge.

"Ha, I'm winning," she proudly says

Her brother climbs down from a tree. "You're only beating me by one. Quick hide, there's another elderly couple coming this way."

"Well be quick, we gotta be home soon, Mum needs help with the lunch."

In the Sink

"Daddy, there's something in the sink."

"Just turn on the tap."

Sandy turned the tap on. "Daddy, it's still there."

"Turn both taps on."

She turned both of the taps on. "Daddy, it's still there."

"Have you turned both taps on to wash it away?"

"Yes, but it won't go away."

"Just leave it and go to the toilet. It'll go away when it's ready."

Sandy looked at the sink then at the toilet, which was right next to each other. "But Daddy, I don't want it to watch me on the toilet."

"Okay, I'm coming, it's just a spider. It can't hurt you."

Sandy stepped to the side and allowed her father to enter. "Daddy, I don't think it's a spider."

"Holly—"

Inside the sink sat a green gremlin licking its lips.

"Jesus—what the—" he whispered, picking up a bath towel.

It jumped out of the sink and latched onto his neck.

"I can't wait any longer. I'll just use the toilet downstairs," said Sandy.

Is She Dead?

I sat beside her body, it was covered in blood. Jenny sat behind me and sobbed quietly. I inspected her lifeless body. There was definitely no sign of life; her eyes seemed to glaze over.

"Is she dead?" Jenny finally asked.

"Yeah."

"What am I supposed to tell my mum?"

"It was an accident. I didn't mean it," I said, wiping the blood off my hands onto my jeans. "At least she died quickly, it's not as if she suffered."

Jenny crawled up beside me. "Where's the knife?"

"I threw it over there." I pointed to a plant pot.

"We need to hide the knife and her," Jenny said, biting her nails.

"What for? It was an accident."

"No one is going to believe throwing a knife at her was an accident."

"Well, it's not as if I was aiming for her. I was aiming for the apple on top of her head. She shouldn't have moved."

Jenny looked at her watch. "Shit, mum will be here soon with the kids."

"Just tell her that her dog has ran off and I'm looking for it."

"What about the mess!" She motioned to the red stain across the grass.

"Keep her in the front room. I'll clean up out here."

"But what … how, are we going to explain about her dog being dead?"

"Don't worry, I'll tell her she was ran over."

"She won't believe that."

"She will when I throw the dog under a passing car."

Jenny paced the garden. "From now on we're sticking to

the bow and arrows."

Claire Nixon, born on the unluckiest day of September 1973, is from the North-East of England. She is the mother of five children, six if you include her husband.

She started creating short stories and poetry a few years ago, inspired by her regular reading. Now she spends some of her spare time writing in many different genres. She's currently a full time student through Open University aiming for a BA in Literature.

She has had several short stories published in magazines, e-zines, audio and anthologies. In December 2004, she published her children's tale 'Tabitha and Pirate Jim' as a present for her eldest child, Tabitha. Tabitha and Pirate Jim is now published as an audio tale with Audio Stories For Kids.

In between writing and studying she is the founder and editor of Twisted Tongue magazine, a magazine that pushes the boundaries.

Chapter 7 … Rachel Green

Not Undead

Gillian Du Point settled herself next to the sleeping form of her lover and drew a ruby-painted fingernail down his cheek. He woke with a start, clapping his hand to his face.

"You minx!" he said staring at the blood on his fingers. "That hurt."

Gillian laughed. "Nothing you can't cope with, Harold," she said. "Want me to kiss it better?" She smiled just enough to show the elongated tips of her canines.

Harold laughed. "That's all right, thank you." He sat up licking the blood off his hand. "Why is it," he asked, "that I like the taste of my own blood but find the idea of drinking someone else's appalling?"

Gillian swung her legs off the bed, the velvet of her coat hissing across the duvet. "It's just a hang-up from when you were mortal," she said. "Then you found the whole idea of sharing body fluids with someone else abhorrent, thanks to the wonders of diseases like hepatitis and AIDS." She shrugged and looked out of the window at the gibbous moon over the fields. "You'll get over it."

Harold dabbed at his face again. "Will I?" he asked. "Do I want to, that's the question."

"You'll have to at some point." Gillian turned back to him. "You may not be a true vampire but you still need huge doses of blood to regenerate tissue."

Harold got out of bed and began to dress. "I have a theory that blood plasma might work," he said. "I could hook myself up to a drip and get it that way."

Gillian shook her head. "That may work if you're convalescing," she said, "but what if you were in a fight? You need to suck it down and get on with the action."

Harold laughed. "I'd rather just avoid being hurt in the first place," he said. "That usually works for me."

Gillian held up his jacket and he slid his arms into it and shrugged it up onto his shoulders. "Not always," she reminded him. "There are times when I've had to feed you myself."

Harold grinned. "That I don't mind," he said. "Drinking from you is euphoric." He pulled on his boots and checked his reflection in the mirror. "Do I look alright?"

Gillian looked as well. Although she stood beside him, only his refection showed. "You look elegant in black," she said, straightening his collar. "Now come. I can smell blood on the wind."

Comfort Food

Felicia growled.

"What's the matter?" Gillian sat up and looked across at her lover. "Are you in pain?"

"You could say that." Felicia looked through the uncurtained window at the night sky. "The moon's coming up."

"Ah." Gillian nodded. Her partner was a werewolf and couldn't help shape shifting under a full moon. "You're going through the change."

"I wish." Felicia growled again. "Why is it that I get my period at the same time that I shift into wolf form? I need comfort food."

Gillian smiled. "I've got just the thing." She went down to the kitchen and returned with a plate, a knife and blue Stilton cheese.

Felicia smiled. "Cheese? You're a vampire. You can't eat it."

"Perhaps not." Gillian pressed her lover back so that she was supine on the bed. She placed the block of cheese on the flat belly and cut off a chunk.

"Ow." Felicia hissed. "You cut right into me there. I'm bleeding."

"I know." Gillian dipped the stilton into the blood. "You'll heal within minutes though." She licked the dark liquid from the white cheese and dipped it again, this time putting it into her mouth

Felicia laughed and leaned forward as her own blood filled out Gillian's lips. "How decadent," she said as the sharp tang of the stilton overpowered the scent of the blood. "I never thought of being a vampire's cheese board.

"I'll suck the blood off," Gillian said, leaning in for a kiss, "and you can eat the cheese."

The Black Death

Jedith held the creature up and kissed it on the nose. It wriggled from the contact, twisting its body left and right in an effort to free itself from her grasp, its tail spinning in cartwheels.

She set it free and it sat on its haunches, using its forelimbs to wash her scent off its snout, whiskers sweeping backwards and forwards with the motion of its arms. Sufficiently clean, it blinked up at her, yellow teeth glinting in the light of the tallow candles.

Rahab laid a hand on her shoulder. "Is it done, my sister?"

Jedith nodded. "It is done. The rats will carry the fleas throughout the length and breadth of the kingdom. All who come into contact with them will die."

Rahab nodded, looking out across the Thames. "Europe too, I should think, if these ships get away fast enough to carry your pets."

"Hardly mine." Jedith spread her dark wings. "Pestilence belongs to the world."

Psychic fair

"I'd like to have my fortune read, please." Harold smiled at the woman behind the table, his hands resting upon her black velvet cloth.

She raised her hand in the air, rings flashing. "The spirits are unclear," she said, her pewter earrings tinkling like razor blades against glass. "I'm afraid I must rest awhile."

Harold's uncle Frederick passed a hand in front of her eyes. "I'm not that unclear," he said. "I might be a ghost but I'm right here."

"Perhaps she meant whiskey," said Jasfoup the demon, lighting a cigar despite the frequent 'no smoking' signs. "We should bring her a bottle of vodka or something..

"I wouldn't take no notice of her," said the lady next to them. "My grand-daughter's got more talent than she has, and she's only six."

"Who are you?" Harold asked. "You look a bit... chronologically challenged yourself."

Her mouth moved as she worked this through, then she laughed. "I'm not dead, if that's what you mean," she said. "I'm just astral travelling. That's my table over there."

"Oh." Harold smiled. "Can you tell my future then?"

The medium looked him up and down. "I expect you'd like a cup of tea," she said.

Rachel Green is a forty-something writer from the hills of Derbyshire in England . She lives with her two female partners, their kids and their dogs. She was the regional winner of the Undiscovered Authors 2007 competition and her book 'An Ungodly Child' will be published in 2009. When she's not writing, Rachel can usually be found with a katana in her hands in

the study of Iaido and Ju-jitsu, or else discussing philosophy with her partners.

Tales of Jasfoup can be seen at _www.jasfoup.blogspot.com_ and _www.leatherdykeuk.blogspot.com_

"Darkness and Shadows" "Abaddon Rising" and "Mono-Syllable," her books of poetry, and "Jasfoup's Dribbles," a book of one hundred 100-word flashes are available from _http://www.leatherdyke.co.uk_

Chapter 8 ... Lyn Evans

Seduction

She had sloe-dark eyes and long wavy black hair. Skin as creamy as a rose's petal and beneath the diaphanous gown which reached her feet, and clung to every curve, a figure that made him gasp.

He blinked. When he looked again she was still there, although common sense told him that she shouldn't be.

She was walking towards him now, tall and slender, sashaying up to him with a tantalising swagger of her hips. He stood up and leant against the hull of his crippled ship. He'd been here on this planet that was barely more than a piece of rock masquerading as an asteroid for three days. Earth days that was, although it seemed much longer. Surely the inhabitants of this forsaken place couldn't be human? Or even humanoid? She was the personification of his wildest fantasies, if he could have created the perfect woman for himself, this would be her.

She held out both hands to him, as if they had known each other for years.

"Peter, you look so lonely, have you been waiting for me?"

How on Earth did she know his name. "Yes," he found himself murmuring, as if his voice did not actually belong to him. "I've been waiting for you all my life."

"Then wait no longer." She slid first one strap of her gown provocatively over her shoulder, then the other, allowing the garment to slide down to her waist, revealing perfect, round breasts that thrust themselves invitingly towards him.

"Come to me my love, I will show you ecstasy such as

you have never known before."

Some considerable time later, she left the lifeless body of the shipwrecked astronaut, blinked her dark, sloe eyes, and shaking herself back to her natural form, lumbered back across the derelict landscape with a flick of her six foot long spiny tail.

Chocolate Kisses

I put my arms around his neck and hold him close for a moment. Then I stand back and gaze into those large, velvety brown eyes. Cummon Harry, you gonna give me a kiss or what?

I've just finished eating a chocolate bar, not that he needs any bribery of course. Harry will kiss me whether my lips taste sweet or not. I guess to him they always taste sweet. We have that sort of relationship.

He parts his lips, showing large white teeth. He presses closer to me. I close my eyes. Swmwwaaaak. "Oooh, Harry, your kisses are just like sugar."

My husband, standing behind me, tuts in exasperation.

"Cummon Luv, he's ONLY a horse!"

Lyn Evans

www.hywelalyn.com
www.hywelalyn.blogspot.com

DANCING WITH FATE available now
STARQUEST: coming from The Wild Rose Press 29 August 2008
Coming soon: CHILDREN OF THE MIST - the sequel to Starquest

Chapter 9 .. Lauren Rogers

On Top of the World

'We're here! We made it!' She stared at the fields spread out before her and turned to Mike and hugged him.

'I can hardly believe it. We really did make it! Wow! And just look at that view!' She spun round 360 degrees and grinned wildly at him.

'You look like you've had one too many!'

'Thanks a bunch! Shut up and look at the view!'

'Really worth it wasn't it?' 'Yes, absolutely stunning,' she replied and smiled at him.

'Best go back now though.'

'I do just need to adjust the aerial though, love. If you remember that's why we came up here!'

Weekend Waistcoat

'I'm not we'll find anything suitable, sweetheart.'

'But Edward needs something special to wear to the wedding too…'

'I know, Elizabeth but…'

'Please can we keep looking, mum?'

'OK. How about this shop?'

They began to peer at the shelves and racks as they had done in the last five shops.

'Can I help you madam?'

'Oh. I'm not sure.'

'Are you looking for anything in particular?'

'We need something for Edward to wear to a wedding,' Elizabeth said.

'Edward?'

'Yes, Edward. Just here – look.'

The saleslady smiled. 'Aaah, well I have something very special for young Edward, miss. If you'd like to look at this. It's a special weekend waistcoat and it would be perfect for the wedding you refer to.' She held her hands up and twisted them about.

'How much is it?' Elizabeth's mother asked.

'Well madam you're in luck because today it's free!'

Elizabeth gave a little skip of joy and reached up and grabbed her mummy's hand. 'Edward loves it mummy! May we have it?'

'Of course darling. He'll look lovely in it.'

The saleslady gave Elizabeth the carrier bag and winked at her mother. 'Have a good time

One Last Time

'Come on darlin'. One last time. Go on…' he looked her up and down.

'No.'

'Go on. Ya know ya wanna.'

'I said no,' she looked away.

'Come on. You get good money anyway don't ya?'

'The answer is no.'

'But we want ya to.'

'Really, no. Please do go away now.' She turned her back on him.

'What if we says please?'

'I'm sorry, no.'

'Dunno wot you're so worried about. S'only a bit of fun.'

'It might be to you but to me it's my career.'

50

'Career?! Cor blimey. You're havin' a laugh!'

'I'll have you know I'm a fully trained personal assistant! I just happen to also have to deal with visitors and, and... contractors like you!'

'Pity you got a job with this firm then ain't it, with your speech impediment. Rank Associates! Oh go on, love, say it again....'

A deal's a deal

He looked out at the plane waiting on the runway. He shivered. The heat from the tarmac wavered as another plane coasted along and taxied to its gate. He wondered again if he should go through with it, but he'd got this far, they'd paid him well and a deal's a deal. The person next to him was munching a pack of *Doritos* and he considered asking him to stop. Rubbing his head he decided to get a cool drink from the vending machine. He pressed the can to his forehead and held it there for a few seconds to ease the pain. Last time he'd down so much Tequila. Well I suppose it would be the last time anyway, he half smiled to himself, cracked open the can and sucked down the drink.

He went looking for another seat. This time he picked one next to an old lady who was reading *The Times* and tried to peer at the headlines, but she twitched the paper away and huffed at him. He leant back in his chair and put his feet on the chair opposite and belched. The old lady folded up her paper and marched off with a, 'Young people these days!' Then he realised there was someone watching him. He took his feet down from the chair and sat upright. He looked at the announcement screens and then quickly back at the man. Yes, definitely watching him.

Picking up his rucksack he decided to take a little walk. It was still another 40 minutes until boarding time. He wandered around the airport, considering his life and his recent life choices. Funny old world really. He tried to ease the weight of the rucksack as it poked him uncomfortably in the back. Why did they give him such a big old-fashioned thing? He decided to go back and sit down again. The 'watcher' was still there and looked up as he approached.

He slumped down in the seat and glanced at the screens again to check his flight hadn't been delayed. No. Just ten minutes to boarding. He felt the old excitement flutter in his stomach and then jumped as he heard the voice.

'Hello, mate. Just wondering if you're on my flight?'

'Dunno. What flight are you on?'

'Oh yes, sorry.' The 'watcher' pointed to his forehead and circled his finger. 'Silly me. The flight to Dubai?'

'Oh, yes I am – are you going to work for Casing Inc. too?'

The 'watcher' nodded with a smile.

'That's great! We can be buddies! Good job they pay well eh? But how *are* we going to cope with no alcohol?'

Lauren Rogers, *lives in the Forest of Dean with her partner and two children. Enjoys writing short stories and flashes. Currently working on two chapters for a technical publication. Member of the internet writing group The Grail and the Cinderford Writing Circle.*

Chapter 10 …. Helen Harvey

Near Miss

"Jason, bring your book to me." Miss Ellis brooked no nonsense. She looked small among these teenagers, but she had pink spiked hair that said "Don't mess with me – I bite!" Jason thought she was a right looker.

Jason put his head down. "I'm doing it now, Miss." The last thing he wanted was to be near Miss Ellis in front of the whole class.

"No, Jason, you will bring it here, now. I'd like to read some of the contributions you've obviously been sharing with your friends." A titter ran amongst some of the girls, Jason was in trouble again.

With as much nonchalance as he could muster, Jason hauled himself out of his seat, sidled between the desks and handed her the exercise book. Miss Ellis glanced at his doodling with disdain. Jason towered over her. He could see down the top of her open shirt; he could see the little ribbon in the middle of her bra, could see a bit of the lace.

He turned abruptly to face the white board; stuffed his hands into his pockets to hide his sudden predicament.

"Jason, don't look away just because you don't like what I'm telling you. I expect more at this level, at your age."

At least she hadn't realised. Jason turned back. Tod and Marty were sniggering at his telling off. Thank God they hadn't realised either.

He watched Miss Ellis tuck a strand of hair behind her ear, keeping order. He noticed the faint flush of annoyance in her cheeks. Being cross with him made her look dead fit. He gritted his teeth, fixed his attention out of the window, thought of trigonometry. But he could still smell her perfume. He shuffled again, then abruptly she handed him the book and he could escape.

But as he scuffed away, she called after him, "And pull your trousers up, I can see half your underpants."

The class erupted in hysterics and door slammed as Jason legged it, scarlet-faced. Bitch! She'd shown him up in front of his mates and she sounded like his mum - and she'd been looking at his arse. Gross! He'd never live it down.

He sprinted round the corner of the music block and barrelled over the English teacher, Miss Perry, sending books and papers flying.

Mind you, detention with Miss Perry wouldn't be a bad thing; she was a bit of a looker...

eBay

Listed in category: Baby > Maternity/ Pregnancy

Two souls on offer; death forces sale.

Soul one: Marked in places, no longer transparent, smudged around the heart. A useful spare, for trade or parts. All offers considered.

Soul two: Barely used, condition as new, still in original wrapper. Priceless.

Delivery not included.

Inner Strength

"He has told me everything," I say, and they make the arrangements. I cannot weep; he must not know.

He lays his head in my lap and I soothe him to sleep, stroking his face, the braids of his hair. His skin is rugged and weather-worn, lined with scars from the battles he has won. I trace them with my fingertips; I feel the breadth of his shoulders against my leg, notice again the bulge of his biceps against his shirt.

And now he lies asleep with his head on my thigh, his soft breath against my stomach. I have tamed the lion, but I love him, the strength of him, the power. A tear falls onto my hand at what I am forced to do. I make the signal; the barber appears in the doorway. I see the flash of his blade and tremble at the fate of our sons. My husband must not wake now or they are lost.

"You must shave off the seven braids of Samson's hair to subdue him."

The barber moves quietly and quickly. The braids tumble one after the other onto the couch where I sit. Then, swiftly, he is gone.

"Forgive me," I whisper to my lover, my husband; and then I call his death to the door, in exchange for the lives of our children.

"Samson, the Philistines are upon you!"

Immediately he is awake. Before he arises, he looks at me. Though he cannot speak without giving me away, his eyes tell me he understands what I have done, and why. He was not asleep.

They seize him, gouge out his eyes; but he is the victor, he has given himself up for his sons.

He loves me still.

Red Balloon

His memories were balloons in his head. They bubbled and banged against his skull, fighting to escape. He had to release them before he could move on.

"Start with the yellow one then, Michael; tell me about the yellow one," Peter said.

"The yellow one. Ah the golden sunny Sunday in the park one." Michael nodded to himself. "Yes, that was a good day. That was the day I first saw Sarah." He closed his eyes, remembering the scene. "She was sitting on a bench and all the daffodils were out behind her like banks of angels." He sighed as the balloon spun away into the heavens.

"And next?"

"The pink one. The cuddly baby skin one. A darling daughter Lucy pink one."

"You have to let go, Michael. There's no going back."

Michael nodded again. Lucy would fly the highest. He hesitated, then said, "Blue. Blue comes next. The colour of arguments and cold silences. A falling out of love. That's easy to let go; I don't want to remember." He shook his head and the balloon was gone. Only one more.

There was a long pause.

"Red now, isn't it?" Peter coaxed. "It usually is in these cases. Tell me."

Michael felt his blood running out of him. He felt the anger of the red balloon, the day he had found her with him. Sarah, with his own brother, laughing and kissing over coffee in the kitchen, while Lucy cried somewhere above in the house. He had snapped, raised his hand to her. And she had grabbed the knife. Stabbed him.

The red balloon burst in an explosion of blood. Michael covered his face and wept. Peter held him.

"The balloons are all gone, Michael, your life is done.

You have done well. Come, come in."

Peter opened the gates and drew Michael into the silver of heaven.

Helen Harvey lives in Harrogate with her two children and her dog. She has a passion for poetry; and since gaining a degree in English Literature with the Open University she has also started writing a novel. Helen is a keen swimmer, and works in a very busy office... so when she's not swimming, she's drowning.

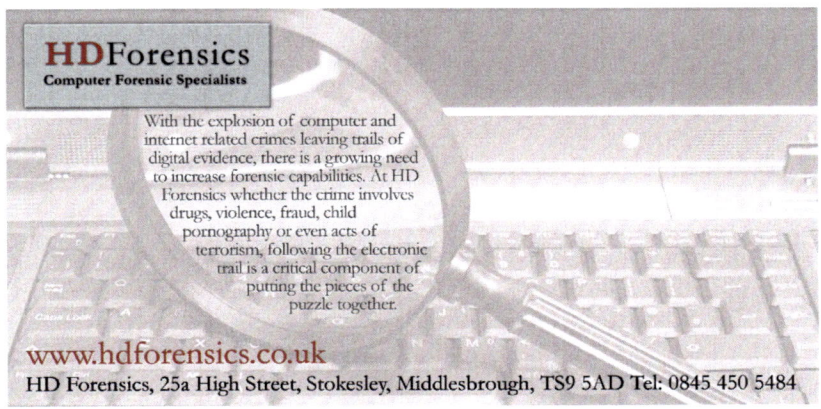

Chapter 11 .. Meg Kingston

One Child Too Many

"How long have you had these feelings of inferiority?" he asked and I tensed, my legs lifting away from the couch.

"I guess it started when I was very young," I answered.

"What's the earliest such event you can remember?"

"It wasn't anything specific. I just knew Mum preferred my two big sisters."

"I thought you were triplets."

"We are, but I'm the youngest. The runt of the litter."

"I wouldn't phrase it like that," he answered. "So the three of you aren't very close?"

"The others are. They were always a pair, and I was the other one."

"When did this start?"

"Mum always said three babies were too many. She wanted to breastfeed, you see."

"I'm sorry, I don't quite understand …"

"You can't breastfeed three babies at a time. You do two, and the other has to wait. One child too many."

Harriet, the Viking Warrior

Harriet straightened her helmet and ducked under the trees, walking on the soft grass to avoid the gravel path that would crunch beneath her feet in their soft leather shoes. She froze at the sound of voices, easing back into the shadows as two men in strange clothing walked past. Oblivious, they didn't notice her; although they passed close enough for her to smell the beer on their breath.

Harriet waited motionless for them to enter the house at the end of the path, then shouldered her axe and made a dash for the heavy, wooden door herself. She raised her hand to strike, but was startled by someone opening the door from the inside. Harriet stared aghast at the caped man in front of her.

"Harry – I didn't think you were coming," said Batman.

Madame Pompidou pushed past him, reaching a hand towards the Viking.

"Just ignore him, Harriet," she said. "Don't let your ex spoil the party for you

This story first published in "Manucript and other stories" by Meg Kingston. Pub: Jay Walker Writing, March 2008

Ostrich

His wife always said he refused to face facts, hid away rather than address issues. She'd repeated this every time she wanted him to do something and he'd tried to evade it.

As usual, he switched off after about thirty seconds today, letting her words wash over him, never hitting home, never touching his heart, passing him by completely. He just stood, his hand on the handle, waiting until her flow had stopped and he felt he could make his excuses.

'Yes, Dear. But I have to go now. Tom is waiting.'

'But weren't you listening? I said …'

He wouldn't have heard the rest, just pulled his coat off the rack and shrugged it on.

She let the letter fall. She'd deal with the oncologist herself.

This story first published in "Manucript and other stories" by Meg Kingston. Pub: Jay Walker Writing, March 2008

Meg Kingston's *non-fiction work has appeared in several specialist magazines as well as better-known publications including New Scientist, Radio Times and Reader's Digest. She has three collections of short stories in print, including many of her prize-winning tales. Her fourth book, a factual account of life with a disability in the 21st Century, will be available in 2009.*
Website: www.JayWalkerWriting.co.uk

The Dragon Bridge

A collection of short stories by
Meg Kingston

ISBN 9780955260216
AVAILABLE FROM
WWW.WORD-POWER.CO.UK

Chapter 12 .. Antony Kane

Cultural Differences Can Kill

When our town was first twinned with Madison in the USA, I didn't think much about it. I certainly never entertained the notion of going there. However, as the years went by first one local firm then another set up over there. To make it in the States, apparently, was the thing to do. That giant market. Everybody wanted to be a giant-killer. Even the council set up an office to encourage it. They didn't seem to notice that it was all one-way traffic, that the Americans never set-up in our town.

The media made it look like one success story after another. Parades, singing, celebrations. Impressed Americans fondling our goods. However, whenever I managed to get my hands on one of these companies end-of-year accounts the numerals told their own story and that story was not in Technicolor but in red, a very bright red: blurred, like a wound that hasn't yet been staunched.

When Ken, my business partner, said we should try *our* luck, I laughed out loud but he was deadly serious.

"It'll be a fresh start!"

"Ken, we are doing fine here where we are."

However, I agreed, against my better judgement, that we could at least check out the market. Ken took seven suitcases, I took an overnight bag and a copy of *Moby Dick*.

We were to be there for two weeks.

At the trade fair, the Americans were very friendly and extremely positive about our wares. You would think they had never seen an electric saw before.

"I've simply gotta have one of them," they'd say.

"Let's do lunch!

Or:

"Would ya look at the size o' that thing!"

Back home, Ken took me out for lunch at the best restaurant in town, *on his own money.*

"What did I tell you?" he said, smiling.

I put the *Moby Dick* up on the table.

"Look at that," I said.

"What about it?"

"What page am I on, Ken?"

He picked up the book, observed the bookmark.

"Is this a trick question?"

"Nope."

"Page seventeen."

"Ken, if I go to the States, I'm never going to read another book, I just know it."

"That's because we'll be so busy selling saws," he shot back at me.

In the end, after much wrangling, I stayed behind to run our operation over here. Ken had a bad first year (the staff weren't right, we hadn't put enough into marketing) and an ugly second year (no customers to speak of, we'd been advertising in the wrong places). In the third year we were sued by a man who had sawed over the branch he had been sitting on. He'd plummeted to the ground, breaking his back and was paralysed from the waist down. Ken was clearly shaken when I talked to him on the phone about it. It could cost us a million, he said.

"That idiot can't sue us!" I said.

"Oh, yes he can. We should have had a picture of a man sawing the branch of the tree he was sitting on in our users' manual and then had a big no-no cross through it."

I burst out laughing.

"Well, that's what you'd expect his lawyer to say," I said.

"It wasn't his lawyer who said it, it was *ours*," Ken returned.

Frank's Dream

Frank was depressed. The previous night he had had a dream in which he found three nappies in a blue carrier bag.

"The worst of it was that I was looking for them," he said.

toc-toc

toc-toc.

Woodpeckers! Turquoise-throated or red-rumped. And my head sore from the over-refined whisky of the evening before. And my ear over-sensitive to the large rooms and elongated passages of this Georgian-childhood home, mansion, apartment building, block-of-flats, poem, whatever it turns out to be. It was dark when we arrived and there were meteorites on the wind.

I sit up just as Cyril sticks his head round the door jamb, a silver tray in his pudgy hands, hands that have not aged: hands that have not receded (as has his hair), hands that have not taken on life-threatening lines (as has his forehead). And on that tray.

"What's with the woodpeckers?" I ask, attempting to kick off an over-sized duvet, succeeding only in kicking up a dust of feathers, small brown things like clues in an old detective picture.

"Woodpeckers? There are no woodpeckers in these parts."

toc-toc.

As if in reply. As though knocking to my defence. And I'm a defensive type, so I'm pleased and to show my gratitude I give off my brightest smile.

"They're not woodpeckers. That's the county cricket team. Their green is water-logged and so Mama has allowed them to use one of the back fields."

toc-toc.

And on that tray, marmalade, glittering, on a bed of butter, spread thinly over a crisp slice of white toast.

toc-toc.

I put a hand to my head. Something rattles inside it.

"Probably that large bone I call my brain," I hear myself say, only it doesn't sound like me, coming back as it does off the lime green walls of this unknown bedchamber. And suddenly I'm afraid. My teeth feel too large and fragile. Exposed.

"I'm not incarcerated again, am I Cyril?"

"No, we're at Mama's," and now it is Cyril who smiles, one of his small, careful, caring smiles.

"Then that argument you had last night, with your father?"

About war. And Cyril standing up to his father, as he has been able to do so ever since the old man took a fall from his horse, cutting him down to size, strapping him to a wheelchair. Half-man, half-statue. Litte more than a bust.

"I'm going to say a bold word now, Father, the barren glory of a military honour."

That almost got the old man walking again. However, it was Cyril's Mama who stood up, showing great grace and agility, and slapped, elegantly, satin-sleeved, her son across the face.

"You have an unlucky tongue!"

Ever since the horse-riding accident, the old man might have lost six legs (the horse was put down and shot) but he has gained two extra, dexterous arms.

"An errant *lapsus linguae*," she had whispered, curtseying by the wheeled, steel chair.

toc-toc.

And Cyril there. Suddenly, in white. Like the light behind the light. The crumbs falling onto a plate, mercifully porcelain. His stick-up collar. A cricket bat in his left hand, Congreve's *Collected* in his right. And he quotes.

"Who would die a martyr to sense in a country where the religion is folly?"

toc-toc

And we laughed, and the laughter tinkled, as the crumbs had done, down onto the porcelain plate. His father stood behind his laughter but Cyril couldn't see that. I'm more fortunate. The only old men I have to carry around are poets and if their overstretched words break, I simply let them flutter to the ground and then pass by.

toc-toc.

(first published in Aesthetica, issue 9, March/April 2005)

Anthony Kane Evans *has had over thirty short stories published in various literary magazines, including London Magazine (UK), The Tusculum Review (US) and Etchings (Australia).*
When not writing he makes documentary films on a freelance basis for the Danish Broadcasting Corporation.

Chapter 13 .. Su Laws-Baccino

Divorce in flashes

I'd had a fun evening. It was good to see everyone, to have a laugh and gossip. The meal was excellent. A bit expensive; no doubt Stanley will moan when he knows how much I've spent, but so what? He's always miserable these days. In fact I hardly ever see him. I don't complain. I'm only too happy to have the house to myself. He goes in and out. I suppose one could say we live separate lives, but perhaps that's part of retirement. This evening my friends were telling me I should divorce him. I'd love to but how could I … he's boring and secretive, like he's always been, but he's done nothing bad.

As I walk up the garden path, I realise Stanley's in … waiting up to interrogate me no doubt.

The door opens before I turn the key in the lock, a uniformed officer greets me, 'Mrs D'eath? Detective Inspector Holcombe.'

I take a step back, 'Yes?'

I'm invited into my own home. Stanley is seated on the sofa; he's even paler than usual. He's wearing his old raincoat and something bright underneath. He says nothing. Looks down when he sees me. I'd know that sheepish look anywhere. 'So what's going on? Anyone going to tell me?'

'Yes, yes, of course, Mrs D'eath,' the officer pauses, he has an irritating cough, 'this evening's Crimefixers programme received a large number of phone calls in answer to one of the programme's photo-fits. Some gave your husband's name and address.'

'But what's he supposed to have done?' My mind was racing. I was irritated, what a horrid end to my enjoyable evening, 'Stanley?'

'Would you like to tell your wife, Mr D'eath?'

'I've confessed, isn't that enough!'

I've never seen my husband quite so humbled. It was difficult not to smile. I didn't feel sorry for him. It was refreshing; he was getting a piece of his own medicine. He loved putting people down. He was an expert at it. What goes around, comes around.

'So what've you been up to Stanley … robbing banks … some excitement for once?' I was beginning to enjoy his wretchedness.

A policewoman moved forward from the shadows and pulled out one of the dining-room chairs, inviting me to sit. I ignored her, 'Well go on then … someone … put me out of my misery … Stanley?'

The Detective Inspector, almost choking now, continued, 'Er, it's like this, it would seem that he's been loitering in Love Lane, down by the Bingo Hall,' he pulled a large white handkerchief from his pocket and wiped his streaming eyes, 'dressed in a frock and flashing at the women as they leave the sessions.'

A few moments of silence until I burst out laughing, 'Well that's it then Stanley … I've had enough … I'll pack your suitcase.'

I continued to laugh long and hard as I climbed the stairs. This was much easier than divorce.

Pacifying Pleasures

It was 8am. I was running late. I'd been on the phone too long. Everything was fine until I got his text to say he couldn't make it this evening. How could he do that to me?

I'm so disappointed, so fed up.

I growled at the dogs as they criss-crossed in front of me twisting their leads as we made our way round the usual route. The delicious smell of newly baked bread wafted across the field from the Coop; dark roasted coffee was being served at the b&b; and that special British aroma of bacon and eggs met me as I turned the corner. I imagined the guests sitting down to their meal … finished off with lightly browned toast, without crusts, homemade marmalade and butter curls.

I fought to dispel these inviting thoughts from my mind as I trudged the perimeter of the field wondering what I would do that evening, alone. On my way home, passing the b&b again, I heard fresh sounds - of clean cutlery being laid; and a washing machine whirring away; the 8.30 news on a radio, and the postman was ringing their doorbell.

Arriving home, I popped the dogs in through the door, grabbed my purse and ran down to the Coop where I filled a basket with chocolate, biscuits, cheeses, sweets, buns and all kinds of forbidden foods ready for a siege - an evening on my own.

The day was suddenly inviting.

How Many?

Admiral Barnaby FINCH, RN
Sunday 16 October 2005 11am
The Angel Room

Claire was late. She rushed through the foyer to the designated room, and as requested, handed a copy of her birth certificate to a receptionist who registered it as number 58, invited her to take a seat, and then crossed to close the main door.

There were still no clues as to why or who had called the meeting. It was a mystery. Why would anyone be calling a reunion in her father's name?

There were many men and women standing around; all looking mystified. No one spoke. Photographs and documents adorned the walls. Claire took a look – the photos were of her father at different stages of his life; the documents too, each one recorded some piece of his short life - 30 years.

A whisper of 'hush' went round and the room fell silent as an elderly gentleman took to the stage. He glared over a large moustache, booming loudly he announced, 'Ladies and Gentlemen, or should I say, Sisters and Brothers, it would seem that we have something in common … a father … Barnaby Finch no less … quite a lad, wouldn't you say … 58 of us present and who knows how many more around the world!'

The family group gasped in disbelief.

Lonesome

Morning mist softens, a new day is born.
Gossamer clouds swirl, curl around the sun
as it dances on leaves, shimmering tears.
A veil of pale violet cuts shadows,
rests on walls dripping with dew,
stifles echoes and images of death.

Day flashes by. I wait.
I sense she's awake, return her faint smile.
I move closer, listen for heartbeats,
rhythm of breath; and I long to look
at her cerulean eyes, so tightly closed.

Sobbing, as all that I love slips away,
I hold her limp hand,
brush her cold lips with mine;
feel the last tremors. And, as the moon
sends darkness to destroy my dreams,
I shriek silently, 'Why her?'

I carry her onto the beach,
lay her carefully on the white sand
and wait, wait for the tide to come in.

Painted Storm

A sulking summer breeze disturbs the stifling heat.
Above us, spinning lazily in this zephyr,
in time with the rhythm of the heavy rain,
a snappy silver light; a crystal, playing shrilly
in rainbow hues on closed casement windows.
Hundreds of rivulets chase, meet, and merge.

Cars glide by, sometimes sinking in hidden
rain filled potholes; eerie grey spectres
behind a curtain of rain-fused glass, faces
distorted, vacant, staring blindly. Frothy,
cream kapok clouds threaten: briefly move
the mauve clouds hiding the steely sun,
before lightning wipes it out -
a watercolour in the throes of birth.

Bamboos dance hysterically in a sudden

strong wind boldly trumpeted in with thunder;
and the downpour hits the scorched brown earth,
flushing fast-flowing gutters, kayaking rubbish
and dirt down the empty road, a river.
An umbrella collapses, its owner sprints, soaked,
in the direction of home. Slugs and snails treacle
on the green fungied wall, graphic designs
left in their wake, mimicking the patterns
on the panes. Blankets of rain scour the tarmac
roasted by months of tropical heat, then rise
and cover the road in geyser-like steam.
Mesmerised, rocking in rattan, we patiently
await the death of this much-needed storm.

The Duchess Exits

Carried high by swarthy young
men, slowly she threw lasting love
at the world, to her friends.

Draped in favourite purple
pashmina scattered with blooms
and fallen petals that moved

in the creases; then, blown by the wind,
found the sand and pebbles
that led to the church and the choir.

Her gaze caught the glint of sun on spades'
blades. She was grateful to old lovers,
the men who dug her grave.

 **Poetry and Prose and Cover Art by Su Laws Baccino**

Just Su
Price: £4.99

More Su © 2007
Price £5.99

Poetry and Prose and Cover Art by Su Laws Baccino
A book of poetry and prose endorsed by one of the UK's favourite poets, UA Fanthorpe, who says: 'There is something about Aldeburgh. We already have the works of Crabbe the poet and Britten the musician. Now we have another poet and storyteller, who catches the subtle moods and understands the magic of the Suffolk coastline and countryside. Su Laws Baccino writes like a painter, her close observation and arresting descriptions efficiently re-create events and surroundings, and draw us, fascinated into her very special world.'

'Su (Baccino)... writes like a painter; her close observation and arresting descriptions efficiently re-create events and surroundings, and draw us, fascinated, into her very special world.' *UA Fanthorpe*
Su was amused when described as, 'an artist, poet and writer'. More like, 'a rebel turned eccentric', she replied.

(advertised anthologies available through Cormorant Publishing Hartlepool)

Jane Flynn

A reflection on one crime, and how it led to another

The stalk of the first flower snapped at its base, emitting a damp, earthy smell. Fuelled by blind anger, I pulled at the flowers, throwing them behind me in a shower of dark loam. Some came free with the bulb intact, others snapped off at the heads. It mattered not. They all received the same treatment. I hurtled around the garden uprooting every plant in my path and flinging them across the lawn. Then suddenly my anger vanished and I was left with nothing. Emotionless I surveyed the scene. Red petals were scattered over the crushed and broken stalks. Their blood, spattered over the soil that had given them life. I was the destroyer. The demolisher. The slayer. I ran.

***

It had started in the playground that morning before school had begun. I was in my 'hot' spot on the black bins. The playground didn't exist for me. I was in my own world, inventing new adventures for my current hero Jack, and his canine companion, an enormous Newfoundland named Butch. Gradually I became aware of a gathering around the bins. Like a chameleon, I blended into the circle to see what was happening. They were all girls – one held paper, a notepad with pp of different pastel colours. She was showing it to the rest and, with oohs and ahhs of appreciation, they admired it. I can see it now; sheet after sheet of untainted colours, clutched in her perfectly manicured fingers. I wanted that paper. No, I needed it.

***

The classroom: Miss Benson was addressing us, her tone serious. No one coughed. No one fidgeted. There was an air of shocked and righteous indignation.

"So someone," she paused for dramatic effect, "must have come back inside during playtime and taken the notebook from Lyndsey's tray."

Innocent wide eyes exchanged glances and shrugs. I joined in. Were my eyes innocent enough? Wide enough?

"I am going to give the perpetrator two minutes, two minutes to come forward to my desk and own up to the theft."

We sat out the two minutes in absolute silence. Any whisper or shuffle might have implied guilt.

"Right, girls first, pick up your bags and line up over there."

Miss Benson started at one end and Mrs Probert, the remedial teacher, at the other. I stood four girls from Mrs. Probert's end of the line and there was nothing I could do but watch her closing in.

She tipped my bag onto a nearby desk. The notebook landed next to a bruised apple. A collective sigh of shock and relief moved around the room like a Mexican wave. My name was whispered in conjunction with another: thief.

Mrs Probert looked at Miss Benson and smiled with satisfaction: good work, a job well done. It was that smile that gave rise to my second crime of the day.

Mrs. Probert loved her garden, and I knew where she lived.

The Red Balloon

Tom's fist clutched the string and the red balloon bobbed and danced in the breeze. With his other hand he held his sister's fingers as she hurried along the path. He felt a bit as if he was her balloon, and she was dragging him behind her on the string that was her arm.

"Hurry up Thomas," she said.

Georgie was cross, but Tom didn't know why. He'd been good at the park, had come away when she'd told him to. Now she yanked his arm to make him hurry and it made him jerk the balloon so that the string dividing them went suddenly slack and the balloon hurried closer to him, as if worried that it too might be in trouble.

They reached the park gates and Georgie turned right, away from their house.

"Where are we going?" he asked. Tom had had enough now; he was tired.

"Just come with me. And hurry up."

Tom tried to hurry, but his legs were only short and he tripped over a paving slab. Georgie yanked him up and carried on, without even looking at his knee.

"My knee hurts. It's bleeding. I want Mummy." He began to cry.

Georgie paused. She softened her voice a little, "Come on Tommie, we're nearly there. I'll get you an ice cream on the way back."

They turned into a garden. A big boy was kicking a ball against the front window, which had boards over it. Tom didn't like the way the boy looked at his balloon.

"Is Blue in there?" Georgie asked the boy.

"Out back."

Without knocking, Georgie pushed open the door. It was dark inside and Tom tightened his grip on the string of his balloon. Georgie seemed to know where she was going. She kicked a door at the bottom of the uncarpeted stairs and it opened into a room which smelt of wax.

A man with a shaved head was leaning over a table. He looked up when they walked in.

"Where the ****! did you get to?" Georgie demanded. "I was waiting. I need a fix."

She shoved Tom in the chest, and he toppled backwards into a corner. "Keep out the way." She said to him.

Tom held the string of his red balloon, while he watched the man fixing his sister. Maybe she wouldn't be so cross when she was fixed. Maybe she really would get him an ice cream.

The man called Blue put a needle in Georgie's arm. She smiled briefly but then flopped onto the floor like a rag doll. Blue tapped her face a few times, but she stayed on the floor.

He looked at Tom.

"Nice balloon." He said. Then he walked out of the room.

Tom waited a long time for his sister to get fixed. But she stayed on the floor. She didn't move. Tom was tired. Holding tightly to the string of his balloon, he curled up on the floor beside Georgie. He went to sleep. When they woke up she would get him an ice cream.

Learning the Steps

It was a strange and emotional experience seeing her upright for the first time in her five year life; feet down on the ground where God intended them to be.

"Lucy," I whispered, "that's amazing!"

Lucy raised her head. It took a great effort, but her eyes met mine.

"You can do it," I whispered.

Liz, the physio took hold of Lucy's left ankle and moved her foot forwards. She did the same with her right foot,

"This is called patterning." She commented, as she moved Lucy's left foot again. "It helps Lucy's brain develop the pathway that tells her to take steps."

I watched my daughter, strapped into her new walking frame, as her feet were "patterned" to walk.

"That's probably enough for one day," Liz said after several minutes. She stood up and rubbed her back. "Lucy will be very tired."

Lucy grunted and I watched her jerk her head up once more. She looked into my eyes and blinked twice: No.

"Wait!" I said to Liz, "Just a minute."

Lucy was very still for a second and then jerked her left foot forwards. She paused again, as if to gather her energy then thrust out her right foot. The wheels on the walker turned.

Lucy was walking.

Granny

I used to love the evenings spent sitting on Granny's lap watching the flames lick around the logs in the fireplace. Everything seemed all right then, perfect even. She used to tell me stories about her wartime childhood, about the soldiers who were billeted on them in their big country farmhouse.

"Those were idyllic days for me, Rachel," she smiled at the memories, 'the soldiers called me their 'pretty little angel'. Everyone else was worrying about the war, and the future of the world, and there was me riding high on the shoulders of my favourite soldier."

"What was his name granny?"

"I can't remember. Isn't that funny, I remember his eyebrows – bushy they were, and they met in the middle, just above his nose. But his name…no."

I would drift to sleep as the fire died down, sometimes half-waking when granny laid me on my bed, to watch as she pottered about, tidying the camp and banking up the fire for the night. Just before she lay beside me every night she would whisper prayers up to the stars. They always ended with the same words.

"Tomorrow, Lord. Please let someone come tomorrow."

I don't remember noticing her ageing as it happened – You don't when you're with somebody all the time. So it was quite a shock to me, waking up at dawn one morning to find that Granny had become an old woman.

I stretched out a hand and stroked her matted grey hair, and she opened her eyes. They were pale and watery. I traced the lines on her face with my fingertips. She smiled at me, and eased herself out of bed to tend the fire and heat the water. In the weeks that followed, I tried to help out more. I gathered wood and fruit, and learnt how to keep the fire from going out during the night. Granny taught me how to catch the fish that basked in the warmth of the shallow water on the shoreline with a homemade spear. She showed me how to weave from reeds containers that would hold water. And each morning I rose first and collected the spring water from the stream.

One morning she was still in bed when I returned with the water. She was still in bed when the water was hot.

"Granny." I gently shook her by the shoulder. Her head flopped to one side.

That was three days ago. Now I sit beside the fire, watching the flames lick around the logs, wondering how I can live here all alone. I lie down on the bed that we had shared and whisper prayers up to the stars.

"Tomorrow, Lord. Please let someone come tomorrow."

Jane Flynn lives in Boston Lincolnshire with her husband, four children and a varied menagerie. She is a teacher, and has enjoyed writing since she was a child. She has had stories and articles published in various magazines and also writes regularly for her church magazine.

Chapter 15 … Paul Zealand

One Child too Many

What I get up to behind the cubicle door with the dog-eared girly mags is well-known to anyone outside, but I'm not doing anyone any harm, am I? After all, in an overpopulated, overheating world every extra mouth to feed and car to fuel is one too many. My conscience is clear as I give people hope, which is a wonderful gift.

Do the staff mind? I should hope not! I'm paying their wages, in a manner of speaking. White gold, it's called these days. Fifty quid a shot – or should I say spurt – since the free donors were scared off by the waiving of the anonymity right. I mean, who wants a steady trickle – no pun intended – of spotty eighteen-year-olds knocking on the door and saying, 'hi Dad.' Some reward for providing a public service.

I get three hundred quid on a good day, but it means a fair bit of travelling and some skill with the art of disguise. The clinics don't like too much repeat business. It doesn't give enough variety in the gene pool – I love these liquid metaphors! – but providing I'm not too obvious I get away with it.

Best thing I ever did, that vasectomy.

No Need to Panic

Stan listened to the clack of typewriters and swallowed hard. That was all the sound was. Nothing more threatening than an office full of harmless, typing women wearing high-buttoned blouses and long . . .

It didn't work, so Stan thought of his rural home, the quiet village on the edge of a forest from which the rattle of busy woodpeckers could be heard. Woodpeckers. Insect eaters. Safe . . .

'Right lads, up we go.'

Stan opened his eyes, the rattle of equipment and clicking of bolts broke the spell of an imagined rural idyll, but as he climbed the ladder the sound flooded back, resembling heavy rain on his cottage roof. The memory linked to that of Elsie, running naked in the rain this summer, laughing as she splashed though the puddles in the deserted forest glade.

He smiled. That was a good image. He walked, as instructed, still with closed eyes as the hailstorm of machine gun bullets ended his life.

Is She Dead?

'Hello darling.' Jim greeted me the same way as always. His tired face lit up and brightened the room. I remembered telling him once that when he smiled the sun always came out for me, whatever the weather. He followed up the greeting with a hug that took away my breath. 'I've missed you. Why have you been away so long?'

'I haven't. I mean it wasn't that long.' I tried to laugh off Jim's concern, but he was too sharp.

'What's wrong? It's Anna, isn't it?' He panicked now, a vague memory triggering the automatic reaction. 'Where is she?'

Should I lie? I asked myself that question every day. Today, as every other day, I knew I couldn't.' 'She died, Jim.'

'No! How . . . What . . . She can't . . .'

And so it started again. The grief and horror of it all. Both of us re-living our daughter's death on her backpacking holiday. Jim couldn't remember anything more than ten minutes in his past. I could forget none of mine. He was damaged by a rare virus soon after Anna's death. I am cursed with an overactive memory. Between us, we share the torment every day.

Weekend Waistcoat

Every child needed one, so Ben asserted. His mates all had one, so why couldn't he? They wouldn't let him go with them any more and it was so unfair!

I sighed.

'Listen to me, son. Do you know what an arms race is?'

''Course I do. Who has the most nukes.'

'Well, it's not just about nukes. It applies to the street, as well.'

'Whatever . . . '

Sometimes I wanted to shake him, even give him the threat of a "good hiding" used as a reasonable deterrent by an older generation than mine. 'You push someone, he pushes you back. So then you thump him and he thumps you. You thump him again so he pulls a knife. You pull yours then his mate takes out a gun–'

'But that's crap, dad. I'm not going to start on anybody! It's for self-defence.'

'Stay out of trouble, nobody can catch you if you run!

'Like a coward.'

I was getting nowhere. It was time for the planned compromise. 'Look, hang on a minute.

I fetched the box from my workshop. The contents only weighed a few ounces so the box felt empty in my hands.

'Here.' I held up the waistcoat. 'I call it the Weekender.'

'It's Kevlar and perforated ceramic. I'm developing it for use by the police force as a lightweight, stab and bullet-proof vest to be worn under normal clothing. A bit like rugby pads, but lighter. You wear this and you'll be safe. Also . . .' I took a short tube out of my pocket and flicked my wrist downward. An eighteen-inch length of metal telescoped out. 'This is an asp. You aim for the wrist holding the knife. So no knife, but no need to run away either, okay?'

'Yeah, cool.' Ben looked relieved. Face was saved. I'd done the best I could – short of locking him up in a safe place.

Near Miss

'Will Michael Price, aged four years, please report to the nearest security station. His family is looking for him.'

Part of me was angry in a way. Not at the situation – I couldn't believe my good fortune as I listened to the tannoy – but at the sheer incompetence of the announcer. What four-year-old is going to know where, and what, a "security station" is?

The little boy I had my eyes on was obviously alone. He stood in a corner made by an outhouse and a Portaloo, looking as if he was waiting for somebody, but with that recognisable sag to the shoulders characteristic of a lost child. Nobody else was paying the slightest attention. A sudden rush of people in the direction of the runway meant that the air show was about to re-start with another noisy fly-past of military jets. Who had time for a little lost boy? That was
somebody else's problem, not the paying customers'.

'Hello, are you Michael?'

The boy looked at me. Wary but desperate to be found. His bottom lip quivered.'

'It's okay Michael. Your mum sent me to find you. She wants me to take you to her. Would you like that?'

`Michael didn't respond for a full ten seconds, then fat tears welled in his eyes and he nodded.

'Come on then, little man. Let's get you to her.'

He took my offered hand without any more hesitation and my heart leaped. I knew today was going to be good. It had felt like that when I woke up.

The tannoy crackled again and another male voice spoke.

'Michael. Michael? Can you hear me? It's daddy.'

'That's my daddy!'

'Well, he'll be with your mummy too.'

'No!' He screamed and pulled away from me.

'Michael. If you can hear me, please just go and ask a policeman for help. You know, a man dressed like your uncle Neil.'

'My daddy isn't dead! I can hear him!'

Oh hell, this was going pear-shaped. I forgot my plans and turned to go.

'Is there a problem, sir?'

Two police officers blocked my way.

'I was trying to help this little fellow . . .'

'You look familiar to me, sir.'

I broke away, running as fast as I could. I was rugby-tackled within ten yards and lay there face down on sun-dried grass as the cuffs were snapped on.

'He said my daddy's dead, like my mummy. And he's not! I think he's a bad man.'

'We think so too, but let's get you back to your dad, eh?

Chapter 16 .. Marit Meredith

The Accidental Felon's Plea

Trials and terrors (no,
not written in error); terrifying
trials, testimonies to a deed done
down the line (felon found,
no longer free).
Not a minor deed, they said,
no little fine.
I didn't commit murder, nor maim.
I merely took what wasn't mine.
I chomped the children's chocolate,
bow my head in shame.
Will you forgive and forget
if I promise
to re-pay my debt?

The Letter

Tom watched his daughter through the kitchen window, marvelling at her achievements. Despite the slight awkwardness of her movements, she climbed the ladder up to the tree house without too much trouble. He watched as she settled her back against the trunk of the old oak, a big smile spreading across her face. Jessie was in her favourite place, no doubt surrounded by her imaginary friends.

It had been difficult to resist the temptation to wrap her in cotton wool after her rocky start in life, but they had made a concerted effort to allow her to do what most other children do, as far as possible.

Ruth threw Tom a worried look. 'What do we do now? Do we tell her?' She carefully folded the letter she had been reading and re-reading. She'd been dreading this moment, wishing she could turn the clock back, re-run Jessie's early years; hold on to her a little longer. Her eyes welled up. 'I'm not ready for this, Tom. I feel lost already.'

'Come on, Ruth. We have to tell her sooner or later. Please don't let her see that you are upset. You know how sensitive she is. She'll know something is up straight away.'

He turned round to see Jessie standing just inside the back door.

'Tell me what, daddy?'

'Never mind, my little sweetheart. It's nothing really.' He smiled, hoping to reassure her.

'What's wrong, mummy? Why is mummy crying?'

'I'm not crying, silly.' Ruth quickly wiped her eyes with the back of her hand. 'I think it's the onions.'

'I can't smell onions.' Jessie looked at her with wide eyes. 'I'll kiss you better.'

Ruth squatted down to face Jessie, and Jessie held her mother's face between her two chubby hands, kissing her nose.

'I love you, mummy. Are you better now?'

'Oh yes, I'm definitely better now.'

'Ok, then.' With that Jessie was gone, back in the garden, playing make-believe games with her make-believe friends.

'We have to be a little more careful, Tom.'

'What do you mean?'

'We've got to keep our voices down. She might hear us.'

'I doubt if she'll be able to hear us from the bottom of the garden, Ruth. Besides, she's having fun. I'll keep an eye on her, though, just in case.'

Ruth leant against the counter, rubbing her forehead. 'It feels as though every day since the day she was born has been part of a steep learning curve. But she's come so far, overcome so much…'

'Don't you think that's a good reason not to hold her back now?'

'But she's settled and happy, Tom. You know she likes a certain routine in her life.'

'She'll soon enough settle into a new routine, you'll see. It won't be as difficult as you think.'

'I don't want her to feel that she's different from the rest of the children.

Tom looked at her, a furrow between his brows. 'Do you seriously think that she doesn't realise that already?'

'She might just about be aware of it, I suppose. But it hasn't affected her before.'

'Don't assume it will this time, Ruth. Limiting her is not going to do her any good in the long run.'

Ruth nodded. 'You're right. Of course you're right. But it's hard to let her go.' She unfolded the letter, smoothing it out on the table and reading it yet again.

'Who wrote you a letter, mummy?'

Ruth jumped. Jessie had the knack of turning up from nowhere.

'Is it from grandma? Will you read it to me? Please?' Jessie was jumping up and down with excitement. 'Lizzie and Jenny want you to read it, too.'

Ruth gathered her up into her arms, avoiding Tom's eyes. 'It's not from grandma, sweetheart. And you know, Lizzie and Jenny are only your pretend friends. They're not really here.'

Jessie's face changed in an instance, as she thumped her mother's back furiously, with her chubby little hands. 'Oh, yes they are! You are a stupid mummy!'

'Ouch!' Ruth put her down quickly. 'That hurt, young lady.'

'Sorry mummy.' Jessie's eyes were brimming over with tears.

'Come here, you!' Tom lifted Jessie high up over his shoulders. 'Don't cry, sweetie. Sometimes grown-ups don't understand.'

Jessie's bottom lip quivered. 'I know they are my pretend friends really, daddy. But when I'm a big girl and go to school, then I'll have real friends, won't I?'

Ruth and Tom looked at one another.

'Do you want to go to school then, Jessie?' Ruth didn't know whether to feel relieved or disappointed.

Jessie nodded her head vigorously. 'Yes, please! Can I go today?'

'Not today, but very soon. Perhaps we'll go and get your uniform tomorrow.'

'And a pink school bag?'

'I'm sure we can find one of those, too.'

'Well, that was easier than I expected. We didn't even have to tell her about that acceptance letter, did we? But do you really think she'll be all right?' Ruth turned to Tom. 'You don't think she'll feel out of place, do you?'

'She'll have to adjust to a new environment, but that's the same for all the children starting school for the first time, remember.'

'Silly me; in my mind she was the only one to face something new. But still…'

'Oh, Ruth, I know what's going through your mind. She'll need some extra help, sure, but they're prepared for that, you know. Besides, Jessie won't be the only Down's child in the school. They are experienced in coping with special children.' Tom smiled at her, reassuringly. 'And with their worried mums, too, no doubt.'

Ruth dug him in the ribs. 'I'll try to keep a low profile, honest. But, seriously, I like the way you called them special children.' She planted a kiss on his cheek. 'Jessie's not different, is she? She's just our special girl.'

Marit Meredith (aka Anna Reiers) has had comments, articles, poems, true-life stories and short stories published, as well as having work in anthologies published in aid of charities. Visit her website, My Writing Life, where you will find collaborative challenges: www.freewebs.com/annareiers/ www.freewebs.com/theapprenticewriter/ The Pp Magazine, a new literary venture.

Chapter 17 .. Stef Hall

Call to Arms

Take
up your
flag and gun
and march to war
you have no faith in;
scatter your blood, your bone
on foreign soil you can't love,
among the ashes of brothers
who dared too often to think of home.

Breaking Up

You left me standing in the driving rain,
walked away with never a backward glance,
like you had just been waiting for your chance

to leave me there to wallow in my pain,
just a puppet caught in your sorry dance,
you left me standing in the driving rain.

My life is cracked, will never be the same,
set adrift on a sea of circumstance,
drowning, going under without a chance,
you left me standing in the driving rain.

Acres of Sky

Corn husks lay in the dirt between her bare feet, her soles hard and grey from her work, baked into makeshift shoes by the heat of the earth. The chickens scratch as she walks between them with her skirt held high, making a bag to hold the feed she has carefully measured out, making sure there is enough to last until she walks the stone-strewn road to market. The chickens pay her no attention; she is a part of their world, unsurprising and without cause for alarm.

The others pass her on the beaten track between the farmhouse and the road. They chatter like the birds on the power-lines, their many words meaningless and unimportant. None of them speak to her. They don't even notice her: she is as unsurprising to them as to the chickens, and she can't recall the last time any of them thought to play with her.

They are going to school. They think her dull; she was too long in the canal during her birthing, and it has left her too stupid even to write her name. They go to school to learn to go out in the world and make something of themselves, leaving her to work the farm and bring them eggs for breakfast.

She does not mind. They think her dull; but when they are penned in their tiny city flats, their tiny city lives, she will remain, feeding her chickens on her farm under acres of sky.

Mental Health

She was old and tatty in the way of a mouldy old blanket left under a park bench. Her teeth were gone, leaving her breath smelling of rot and dead things; the grime was so deeply embedded in the creases of her face that you'd need a pan-scourer to get it off.

No one could remember when she'd appeared, wandering from bench to bench with her tartan shopper-trolley; it seemed she'd always been there. Mad Aggie, they called her, avoiding the park. If you lingered, Mad Aggie would sit down beside you.

"I'm under the weather," she'd say earnestly, gripping your wrist.

It was clear she was under the weather in her head, at least. No one felt sorry enough to stay. They would pull their wrists from her grasp and hurry away, disgusted by the mucky finger-marks. They didn't see the sunny, toothless smile that crinkled her face with a joy so deep it transformed her into someone you could almost recognise.

They didn't see when she lay down beneath the stars at night, with a lightness of heart she had not felt since girlhood. They didn't see her sleeping soundly for the first time in years, her mind calm and clear at last.

But when they found her body in the January snow, they saw she was smiling.

Rhythm and Blues

The first time I saw Sandy, he was dancing. Eventually I came to realise that was all he ever did, dancing through life like it was a performance; a masked ball and no one would ever see his face because when unmasking time came, he was gone. I think if he'd ever been caught there would only have been an endless supply of masks and no face at all.

He was tall with the typical dancer's physique -- broad shoulders and narrow hips -- and he moved effortlessly. All in black, he drew the eye with his poise. He danced alone, his eyes closed, face uplifted to the flashing lights. He looked transported, as though nothing existed in that moment but the music, the beat, beat, beat of his heart.

His eyes flicked open and towards me as though he could feel me looking. I turned away quickly, but it was too late. His eyes caught me and even at that distance I could see they were green. He crossed the floor towards me. Without a word, we danced.

If I believed in God, I'd swear he'd made me and Sandy to dance together. Every move I made, he anticipated, his slender body rolling with my movements like the tide to the moon. His hands moved towards my waist but he didn't touch. No matter how we twisted and swayed, we never came closer than an inch apart. I thought he was going to kiss me but he shied away, leaving me melting; he had a smile like The Joker, inviting me to come play.

We danced only for each other. No one else existed. When the club closed we carried on dancing, all the way home and into his bed.

He was never mine. I don't think he'll ever belong to anyone. My friends told me they'd seen him with other girls, and he never denied it.

Every time I went out looking for someone else, Sandy was there. Every time I tried to ignore him, he came to me and we danced. We danced and everything was okay.

It took moving two hundred miles across the country to break Sandy's spell. The years passed and I left him in the debris of the past along with broken dreams and regrets; I married, had children, grandchildren and grew old. I sometimes wonder in quiet moments what happened to him, whether he ever found the right dance partner, or whether he danced out the rest of his days alone, lonely. Every time I see a man who can dance, *really* dance, for a moment my heart stops, thinking that it's him.

And when I dream and the years drop from my bones,

firming flesh that went south long ago, there is always a ballroom. There is only one dancer, lonely in the music, waiting for me.

He smiles his Joker smile: come play with me.

Maybe one day, I will.

Stef Hall is a country girl at heart. Born and raised in Norwich, England, she now resides in London with her musician partner, Paul, and their three bonkers cats. She tries to make up for the bustle of city life by procrastinating, walking slowly, and drinking far too much tea. Stef has been writing since she was old enough to hold a pen, but 2007 marked her first  *forays into the publishing world with pieces appearing in Twisted Tongue and La-Fenetre magazines, The Weekly News and a number of anthologies.*

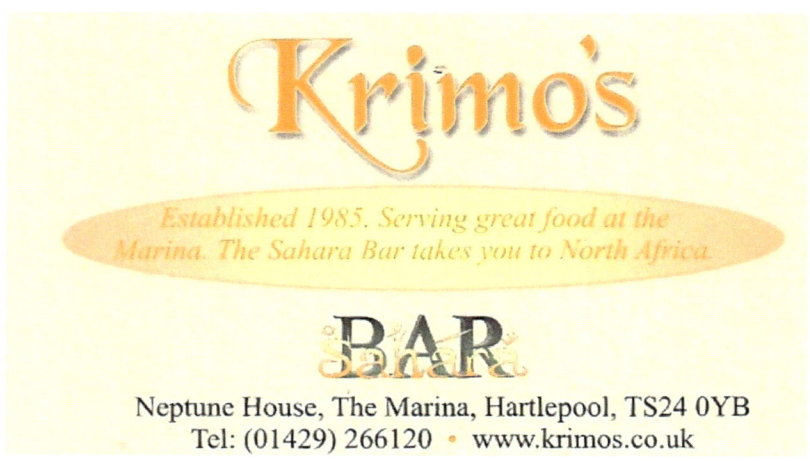

Chapter 18 .. Mia Hopkins

Circles

In the shaded corner of our garden
Where the breeze can not reach
My grandmother sits alone, supported
By a high-backed armchair,
A cane leaning against her side.

Staring toward nowhere,
Her once grey eyes, hiding
Behind cat's eye spectacles,
Are not so steely now;
A liquid blue, forgiving.

Empty, she is full
Of invisible, untouchable air
Where once was substance;
Worn, thin skin caves,
Hollow insides remain.

Though long gone, I see her air
Seep from my mother now; that same
Nose so straight and sharp
It's almost regal.
Or so we like to think.

And there am I, reflected
In her frameless, fragile, shape.
Reminding me that one day
I will become, like her,
Imperceptible. Only air.

Maria Hopkins *was born in Sweden into a family that travelled by force of habit. She lived in seven countries before settling on the edge of a moor in North Yorkshire, where she began to write short stories and poetry. Her first novel, Gardening Secrets, is due to be completed at the end of this year.*

Chapter 19 .. James Hazlehurst

Bon Appétit

Mary looked at the advert in the newspaper, it read: *"The Greatest Diet Ever: Get That Trim Figure you always wanted. Phone now to join the club on: 0898001001."* She placed the newspaper down at the side of her as she sat with her morning toast, tea, bacon, eggs and beans on the lounge table in front of her. She looked down at her stomach. It hung huge and saggy from her like a giant tumour. She hated it. She hated the way it felt and the way that it made her different from all the other women she knew. But nothing she could do would shift it. She had tried everything, she had done the weight watchers points diet, the watermelon diet, the grapefruit diet, the sea food diet and even the Atkins diet, but nothing at all had made her lose weight, in fact a few of them had put more pounds onto here already ample frame. She picked up the phone and dialled the number. After a brief chat to the operator she was surprised to find that there was a club meeting only a mile from her home at the community centre in town. She booked herself in for that following Friday and waited with great anticipation for it to come, "Maybe this is it, the one diet I've been looking for." Mary smiled and got ready for work with an unusual spring in her step.

Friday rolled around quicker than Mary had expected. Since phoning on Monday she had thought of nothing else. She threw her work clothes off the moment she reached her bedroom and got dressed into her best trouser suit ready for her big night, she was so excited she decided to skip dinner altogether. She disappeared out of the house so she could arrive early with her ten pounds membership fee and one pounds weekly submission.

The centre was quite small. Mary was the first to arrive; she walked over to a man standing in the corner of the room looking out of the window.

`"Excuse me sir, I'm here for the slimming club."

He spun round to face Mary. He had a huge smile on his face, "Aaaah yes. You have come to the right place my dear. I'm Ben and I run the slimming course. Please take a seat and we can start, Mary."

Mary did as he asked, "How do you know my name?" she enquired.

"Well my dear you are the only woman to have arranged to come, I doubt that anyone else will turn up spare of the moment, I only had your call all week. I was thinking of cancelling next weeks advert in the paper." He laughed momentarily at this.

Mary looked quizzical, "Surely it's not worth your trouble to deal just with me?"

"Oh nonsense my dear. It's my pleasure. In fact lesson one is for free seeing as it's just you and me."

"I suppose I've got nothing to lose, right?"

"That's right Mary. The only thing you will lose is your weight."

They both smiled at each other and Ben began the advice. He gave Mary amazing advice on dieting, what to eat and when to eat it, how to exercise, slimming pills you can buy, ways to suppress your appetite.

And that is how it went on week, after week, after week. Until one Friday evening…

"Wow I can't believe it," said Mary, "I've lost two stone already and in ten weeks. I don't know what to say. Oh please Ben let me at least pay you for this week's session."

"No, no, no Mary. You must keep your money in your pocket. You are my best and only dieting student and seeing you lose this weight is reward enough. In fact…" Ben paused,

"…let us celebrate. You have done so well I think you deserve a treat. Would you please accompany me back to my house for a meal, it'll be just the two of us as always."

"I don't know what to say," said Mary, "It's been such a long while since someone asked me out."

"Say 'yes' Mary, its only one meal after all, and I promise you the weight will keep falling off."

"OK then Ben, let's do it!"

Mary had always felt uneasy about dates. She was rarely taken out by many men. One time a guy had admitted to her that he was a "Chubby Chaser." Not the most flattering comment she had ever heard, but she blew him nonetheless. The attention of a young and athletic guy like Ben was too flattering to turn down. She smiled constantly in his presence.

Her happiness was obvious to see.

"Please take a seat and I'll get you a drink of white wine…"

Mary sat down and looked around his house, "Are you decorating?" She enquired.

Ben walked in with a bottle of Dry Riesling and two glasses, "Yes, that is right. I don't normally keep these plastic sheets all over my furniture."

Ben placed the glasses down on the coffee table and poured them full. He handed a glass to Mary. "This wine is gorgeous. You know, it goes well with Pork."

Mary took a large drink, "Mmmm it's very good. I can't wait to taste the Pork."

"Aaaah, you will soon enough, but please excuse me while I check on the greens, don't want them boiling dry do we. Please feel free to top up your drink Mary" Ben walked back into the kitchen.

"Are you trying to get me drunk?" said Mary as she gulped down the glass and filled it straight back up.

"No, no, no Mary. I don't want you to get too drunk. It

will spoil dinner.

"Too late," Mary whispered to herself as the room began to spin around and around and around. "What kind of wine is this…… is this……?" Mary mumbled.

The room span faster and faster and faster. Before Mary could speak she passed out.

Mary opened her eyes. The room still was spinning a little and her entire body felt numb. She looked over to her left and sat in an armchair was Ben. On his lap there was a tray and on it a plate of food - a Sunday roast.

"Not going to eat yours?" he said to her as he raised his fork with a huge piece of meat on it and placed it into his mouth.

Mary looked down and there on her lap was a tray and upon it an equally delicious looking roast meal. She reached forward to pick up her knife and fork but could not manage it.

"Ben… Ben… I think I've had too much to drink. I don't feel well."

"That'll be the drugs in the wine I gave you." said Ben as he took a second huge mouthful of meat and placed it into his mouth, "Now are you going to eat yours like a good girl. Remember what I told you, you cannot starve yourself to lose weight, you still have to eat. Now tuck in."

Again Mary tried to pick up her knife and fork and failed. As she struggled with her meal she felt something warm running like water down her stomach. She placed her hand into the gaps between where her shirt buttoned, and she felt blood.   "Where are my breasts?" she said in a groggy, weary voice.

Ben held up yet another forkful of meat, "I told you that I'd keep the weight off didn't I Mary."

As Ben continued to eat Mary passed out.

James Hazlehurst lives in Bilston near Wolverhampton. He has been writing for nearly ten years but has only taken it seriously for the past five. He has several short stories published in magazines and is the interviewer for Twisted Tongue magazine.

www.jameshazlehurst.com

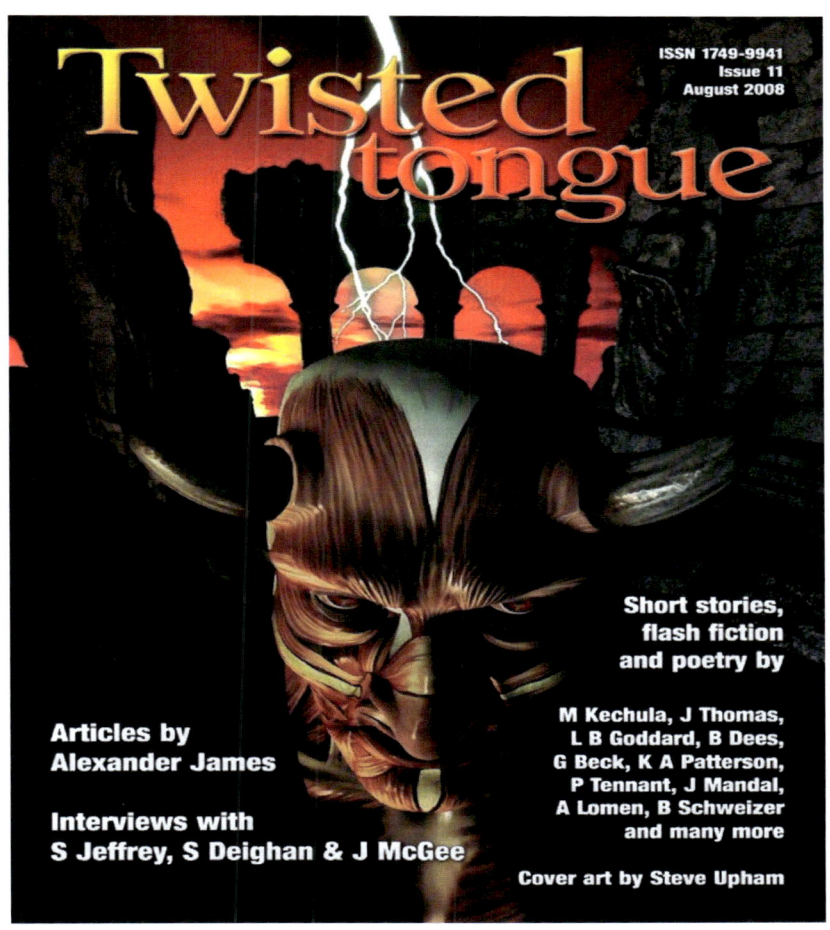

ISSN 1749-9941
Issue 11
August 2008

Twisted tongue

Short stories,
flash fiction
and poetry by

M Kechula, J Thomas,
L B Goddard, B Dees,
G Beck, K A Patterson,
P Tennant, J Mandal,
A Lomen, B Schweizer
and many more

**Articles by
Alexander James**

**Interviews with
S Jeffrey, S Deighan & J McGee**

Cover art by Steve Upham

Chapter 20 .. Jonathan Pinnock

Interior Design

When he acceded to the throne, Emperor Sen's first act was to round up his father's assassins and torture them to death, along with several other unfortunates who happened to look like them. Then he summoned the Lord Chamberlain.

"I want the palace re-painted," he announced. "In my favourite colour."

"Certainly, your majesty," said the Chamberlain. "Which is …?"

But the Emperor said, "Just do it."

An interior designer was summoned, and a long discussion took place as to what the Emperor's favourite colour might be. The Lord of the Bedchamber was strongly in favour of blue, remembering that the Emperor had had a much-loved blue soft toy when he was a baby. But the Lord Chancellor felt that green was more appropriate, because that was the colour of the country's banknotes. So the interior designer got to work, and after several months, the palace was decorated in several luscious shades of imperial green.

The Emperor was furious. "No!" he said, stamping his feet. "I want it done in my favourite colour!"

This time, they decided to go for the Lord of the Bedchamber's suggestion, and the palace was re-decorated from top to bottom in a thousand different shades of blue. It was quite the most beautiful interior in the known world.

The Emperor was incandescent. "Get that man in here at once!" he said to the Lord Chamberlain.

The interior designer knelt before the Emperor, pleading to be told what colour he should choose. By way of response, the Emperor grabbed a sword from his nearest bodyguard and cut a deep gash in the man's jugular vein, causing a livid crimson spray to dance in front of his courtiers' eyes.

"That colour," he said.

The Lord Chamberlain grimaced. Kids could be such bastards sometimes.

Interview with a Zombie

Yep, that's usually the first question that people ask, but it tends to skew the conversation a bit if we start off with that one. So ask me somethin' else.

What's it like adjusting to being a zombie? Hmmm. Good one. Well, first of all, I'd have to say that it ain't as easy as it looks. There's the Shuffle, for a start. First time I tried, I tripped up and fell flat on my face. And you don't want to be doin' that too much if you're one of the undead. Bits of you tend to break off if you're not careful. Even when I wasn't falling over, it looked more like I was kind of mincing. And there's nothing more stupid-looking than a camp zombie, I can tell you.

Oh, no, good Lord no. Please don't get that impression. I was only kidding. Undead society is *very* inclusive these days. We have gays, lesbians and every race and creed under the sun. And we're not fussy about obesity, either. We'll have anyone.

Biggest problem? The food I guess. Live flesh is kinda tricky to get used to, and you would not believe some of the arguments people get into about this. Such as? Such as the religious issues. OK, human flesh is not explicitly prohibited by Deuteronomy, but that ain't gonna stop a zombie Rabbi from arguing about it. And you know what they say, two Rabbis, three opinions? Oh, and don't get me started on the Muslims.

No, you're right. It's not as if it's a balanced diet either.

I've had bad skin ever since I've been a zombie, and I'm sure it's because of the lack of vitamin C. I was discussing this with my dietician only the other day ...

Relationships? Sure, we have relationships, why shouldn't we? OK, you might not think we communicate much, apart from the grunting and the rolling eyes thing, but that's just for show, y'know? We're pretty articulate in private. We have feelings. Some of us write poetry. And we're a very sociable lot.

Say what? 'Course we're sociable! Ever see a zombie on their own? No, 'course not. We're always hanging around in a bunch. Trust me: we're lovely people, zombies, once you get to know us.

Is that it? So this is just some kinda five-minute "me and my life" spot for the back pp? You mighta told me, I wouldn't have bothered getting smartened up. Why're you laughing? Anyway, you wanted to know how I became a zombie? Well, you may not believe this, but I used to be a journalist.

Yeah, really – coincidence, eh? And here's another coincidence. Last interview *I* ever did was with a zombie, too. Hey, don't look so surprised – you didn't really expect to get out of here alive? Come on, think about it. I'm a zombie. It's what I do. Now just hold still and stop screaming, OK?

Jonathan Pinnock *was born in Bedfordshire, and - despite having so far visited over forty other countries - has failed to relocate any further away than the next-door county of Hertfordshire. He is married with two children and a 1961 Ami Continental jukebox. His work has won several prizes, shortlistings and longlistings, and he has been published in such diverse publications as Smokebox and Necrotic Tissue.*
www.jonathanpinnock.com.

Chapter 21 .. Sue Newson

Water

I watch you
And my mind drifts far away
Into the Sea of Forgetfulness.
When I am with you
Time floats by
Tossed back and forth
By the undercurrent of your waves.
My thoughts ebb and flow
Transcending the Oceans of Eternity
Like the passing of your tide.
I am sucked into the Whirlpool
Of Abstract Contemplation
And swallowed by an overwhelming desire
To know my own destiny.
I swim in the River of Collective Unconsciousness
And drown in your beauty.
I drink from your Cup of Knowledge
And sap up your greatness.
You are my Elysium
My Heaven under the sea.

Her Eyes Revealed Everything

Her eyes revealed everything
Every teardrop, every motion
Said in an instant
What her body was aching to say.

Words were unnecessary

(For they are the instruments of the naïve)
Irrelevant in conveying
The feelings of the Soul.

Her smile portrayed happiness
But her eyes gave her away.
In trying to mask her pain
She only succeeded in emphasising it.

She was lost in the world of the un-seeing.
Wishing she were far away
In the land of the poster on her wall
Where they look with the mind's inner eye.

Blind to the hopelessness of her existence
She carried on the façade of her life.
Always wishing that one-day it would be different
But knowing it would always be the same.

Sue Newson started writing poetry at the age of 8 and has had a number of her poems published in the past. In the last couple of years, Sue has been heavily involved in raising funds for the Hypermobility Syndrome Association, a charity that is close to her heart as she suffers from a severe form of Hypermobility, called Ehlers Danlos Syndrome. To date she has produced three poetry anthologies.  *"An Awakening of Conscience" features a collection of her own poems, whilst both "Behind the Mask" and "Hope Unbroken" feature a collection of poems written by Sue and fellow members of the HMSA. All three of these anthologies can be ordered via the HMSA at* poetry@hypermobility.org

The Hypermobility Syndrome Association (HMSA) is a charity run by and for people diagnosed with the Hypermobility Syndrome (HMS).

What we do

The HMSA aims to provide support and information to those affected by the Syndrome and to promote knowledge and understanding within the medical community and the public at large.

We hope to assist sufferers to come to terms with the HMS and the distress that it can cause. The severity of the effects of HMS varies with the individual: some have few symptoms others are severely affected. HMS is an 'invisible illness' and because of this we can look well to the outside world but are often in severe pain. Moreover the nature of hypermobile joints combined with frail tissues means that we are prone to injury when performing simple everyday tasks. This opens us to skepticism, particularly by those in the medical profession who know little about HMS. The pain, stress and frustration can lead to depression: thus depression can often be mistaken as the cause of the illness, not a result of it.

We work closely with those in the medical community with a special interest in HMS. Through our newsletters we aim to provide members with updates on the developments and issues within the medical community. As patients we need as much current and useful information as is available.

In turn it is our aim to provide those in the medical community with information about living with HMS. We can provide valuable data for research just by working as group rather than as individuals. Working in a proactive and mutually beneficial relationship with the medical community, the HMSA acts as both a support group as well as a force for advocacy for those with HMS.

Need More Information?

If you would like further advice or information on either the HMSA or the Hypermobility Syndrome, please either write to us at:
The Hypermobility Syndrome Association
19 Clarence Road
Clare
Sudbury
Suffolk
CO10 8QN
enclosing a stamped self addressed envelope

Chapter 22 .. Kirstylee Davies

Hair Die

Scrabbling and dripping water over the side of the bath I reached my glasses. I checked again. It was still there. The wisp of grey standing out proud against he brunette curls nestling against my skin. Of course I annihilated it with my razor then lay back in the suds and took my glasses of again and sloshed the water under my arm pits to wash my breasts. I had to face it, albeit myopically; my figure was definitely going south for the winter and was prepared for a change of plumage as well.

No-one ever tells you that it's gradual. At thirty you can still wear your jeans and a funky top and go out on the pull without feeling out of place. You can dye your hair how ever you want, streaks, high lights, low lights or a choppy cut that makes you look almost twenty-something. Then, one day you realise that you're '*Madame*' and you have to bite your lip to stop yourself screaming after the waiter "*Moiselle*, it's *mademoiselle!*" as you are led to a side table and the napkin is sharply snapped by a practised flick of the wrist to hide your outfit.

The next step is the 'Big Issue' man. I've walked past him every day for two years and bought each new copy of his magazine. If I don't buy one I give him a cheery wave and smile, he replies with "Morning Miss." and usually wishes me a good day. This morning he called me "luv". His eyes slid past me to the skimpy twenty year old with fresh skin who seemed to have central heating built in. It was freezing and not only was she dressed for warmer climes she had a spring in her step and her skinny little arms were goose-bump free. No turkey wings for her, no stray dark hairs freckled amongst the pale fuzz that I learnt to ignore years ago. No dry spots or bruises or scratches where the cat had been overly affectionate. Just smooth silky tanned skin.

I'm obsessed with other women's bodies. I compare them to my own, is she thinner? Is she younger? Does she dye her hair?

Walking into the pharmacy I head purposely for the hair colour section and resolutely scan the shelves for a dye that will work on the bikini line.

Thumb

My right thumb fell off and landed on the breakfast table.

"George, pick that up." My wife sniffed.

I stuck it back onto my hand and gave it an experimental wiggle.

The second time it fell off I was eating my Friday fish and chips.

"I wish you wouldn't do that," she admonished, "It's un -hygienic."

I didn't reply but re-attached the offending digit, eager to finish my mushy peas. My thumb felt a bit loose but stayed in place for the rest of the evening.

As I climbed into bed I noticed my thumb lying in the centre of the carpet. I bent down to pick it up when it wriggled away from me and hid under the dressing table. My wife fetched the vacuum cleaner with a mutter and a sigh.

Today my left index finger fell off.

Poncho

When I was seventy-one I became popular. I was sweeping the leaves off the path wearing my new red poncho, when for the first time the young woman from five houses up stopped to speak to me. Three days later I knocked on her door with a parcel of soft violet wool and a shy smile. The next day she stepped out with a cheery "Hello!" on her way to work. The poncho looked stunning over her black trouser suit.

My doorbell rang regularly after that. More and more orders for young and old alike; I even made a tiny pink one for a new baby. But fashions change, and no one is wearing ponchos today. I sweep the leaves and exchange a smile and a wave, but the doorbell doesn't ring.

Making Sense

I know your smell,
it permeates the sheets
over-riding the heather scent,
comforting.
I borrow your shirt
when I am cold or lonely,
enveloping each pore in the smell of you.
I put my head on your pillow
when you are gone and
inhale so deeply
black spots appear in front
of my eyes. I am loathe to exhale,
to expel you
each dried bead of sweat
my oxygen
to be consumed, my fire,
a craving.
I carry your cologne
carefully measured
drop by drop and I
exult when strangers ask

"What is that delicious scent?"
Good thing my husband has no sense of smell.

Kirstylee Davies is an Industrialist who occasionally publishes short stories instead of concentrating on her PhD. She can be contacted via www.professionalpolishing.co.uk where she lives, along with lots of machines, and where she secretly writes short stories when she should be working.

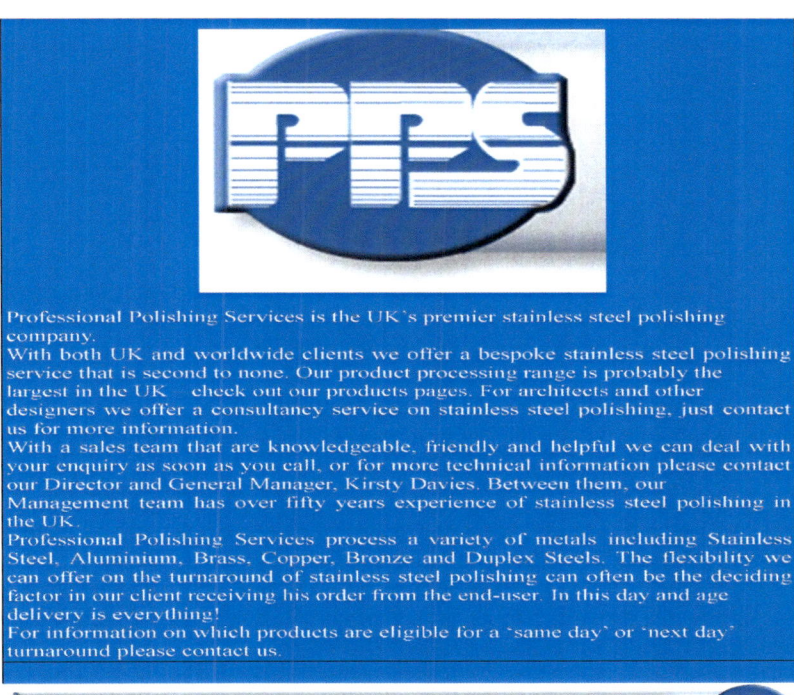

Chapter 23 .. Caroline M. Davies

Dinas gaerog

The only visible remains
of the hill-fort
are two stones

marking where the entrance
used to be. The hump
of the fort is high up

so Owain can see
for miles, down to the blue of the sea
and up as far as Cader Idris.

Hidden amongst the gorse
he can look out, pretend
to be a sentry.

On guard against invaders
but he sees only sheep.
His father never walks

up this way. Owain can steal
away to Dinas gaerog, when he should be
somewhere else.

He's painted the hill
in all her moods.
Watercolour is all he can afford

He longs for oils or a camera

to provide instancy
but the thin paint teaches patience

until darkness drains
away the light; he hunches
back down to the farm. Braced for the never

unexpected impact of his father's fist.
The pictures still alive
inside his skull.

Footnote: Dinas Gaerog is Welsh for hill fort

Not painting by numbers

Owain knows the man in the art shop on the High street must recognise him but he can't help going back. The names of the paints entrance him; alizarin crimson, cadmium orange, and cerulean blue. The trouble is he wants them all. The trouble is one tube of oils would not be enough. His paper round yields him pennies and he needs pounds. But his existing watercolours dry quickly and are easily hidden. Oil paint would leave a tang on the air in the barn for his father to notice. More than anything Owain is afraid of his father finding and destroying his art.

His mother knows. She has a way of discerning what is going on whereas his father is all sound and fury. She will not tell. She has her own secrets to keep, some fancy man for whom she applies lipstick once a week. She returns in the late afternoon with it carefully scrubbed from her face but lit by an inner glory that takes a day to subside before she is back to her mouse self.

Owain pulls up his hood to obscure his face but that makes him conscious of the man behind the counter, watching. 'Perhaps he thinks I'm a shop-lifter', Owain wonders.

"Not buying then?"

"Not today," Owain mumbles.

"Owain," says the man as he is at the door. He freezes at the sound of his name, his heart jumping in his chest.

"Why don't you bring in one of your paintings to put in the window for sale? Then you'll have the money to buy more paint."

Owain turns and looks at the man properly. He is dark haired with the shadow of stubble across the line of his jaw and grey eyes in which Owain glimpses something which might be taken for kindness.

"How do you know I paint?" He asks at last.

"Well you do come in every Friday afternoon..." The man pauses briefly. "And your mother tells me you have a talent for it."

Caroline M. Davies writes poems whenever she can spare the time from work and looking after her children. Her poems and prose have appeared in a variety of print and on-line magazines including Blue Tattoo, Earlyworks Press, Flashquake, Poetry Monthly and Seventh Quarry. Shehas won several poetry competitions the most recent being the JacquiBennett Writers Bureau winter 2007 and the 2007 Blaenau Gwent Poetry Competition.

Chapter 24 .. Paul Harris

Battalion Z

"General, it's a pleasure-"

"I'm a busy man. Just get on with whatever it is you've dragged me out here for."

Professor Dixon gritted his teeth and gave the order. "Begin test, Battalion Z."

Dixon looked out over the firing range. Men stepped out of the bunkers on the range and began to move slowly forward.

In spite of the warning signs, the General lit a cigar. He waited until the first fall of ash hit the floor before he spoke. "Is that it? You hauled me here to watch the most ill-disciplined mob I've ever seen in uniform shamble-"

Dixon held up a finger and glared at the General. "Time to air-strike?"

"T-minus ten."

"Get that finger out of my face, boy."

"With respect, General, shut up and watch."

"If this isn't damn good you can kiss your funding goodbye."

Dixon didn't bother replying. The army brass were always threatening to take research money away, but they never did. They wanted new toys too badly.

The air-strike hit with sudden violence, earth fountaining up on pillars of flame all around the advancing troops. The noise of the explosions faded away to leave grim silence.

"My God." The General's cigar had fallen to the floor. "What the hell have you done, Dixon?"

All Dixon's attention was focused on the range.

The General grabbed Dixon's lab coat and yanked him round so they were face to face. "I'll have you court-martialled for this! Damn it, I'll have you hanged!"

Dixon stared into the man's scarlet face with disdain, then turned his face to the viewing window. "Look, General."

He did, still holding Dixon by his lapels. The sight that greeted him made his fists go slack. Dixon stepped back and smoothed his jacket.

The General's mouth opened and shut silently. When he looked at Dixon again his eyes were wide. "How?"

Dixon smiled haughtily and watched as more of Battalion Z got up and continued to advance.

"What is it, Dixon? New body armour?"

Dixon ignored him. "Have Battalion Z report to the command centre."

"The army will pay millions for this, Dixon."

The General was practically drooling. Dixon knew this was it, the discovery he'd worked all his life for. He was going to be rich and he could finally tell the army to shove it.

"They're here, Professor."

Dixon stepped out of the command bunker, the General at his heels like an eager puppy. The men from Battalion Z stood waiting at attention.

The General stared at them in their ragged uniforms, some of them still smoking from the heat of the shrapnel. "What are they?"

"Soldiers, General. Reanimated and unkillable. Zombies, in vulgar terms." Dixon smiled. "They are the ultimate fighting machines."

The General stood in silent contemplation. "No. They're monsters. And you are an abomination." Dixon reared up in indignation, but his response was killed by a bullet between the eyes.

The General addressed Battalion Z. "This is your final order. Rest easy, men. Rest easy."

Paul Harris *lives in the south east of England with his wife and two young children. He has previously had short stories published in The Parasitorium: Parasitic Sands, The Parasitorium: Parasitic Thoughts (available through Lulu.com) and the SlingInk anthologies Floating, An Angel Passed Through and Footprints (available from SlingInk.co.uk). Paul has also written two novels about a vampiric bounty hunter's adventures in a post apocalyptic world.*

Tall Ships

Mulberry Rise - Hartlepool

Chapter 25 .. Mark Tomlinson

The Fireplace

There was nothing else but a fireplace in that vast and empty room.
As tall as a door and as wide as three and as cold as a Vikings tomb.
I stood against the farthest wall and I gazed at its gaping maw
And I told myself I hadn't seen the things I know I saw.

And I told myself I hadn't heard the things I know I heard.
That there hadn't been a muffled cry or a single shouted word.
I shook my head and I hugged myself and I wished I was not there
While the echo of those phantom sounds still shivered in the air.
While the echo of those phantom sounds still shivered in the air
I shrank against the peeling wall and stammered through a prayer
And then again I saw the scene that chilled me to the bone.
An endless loop of captured time in that empty room alone.

An endless loop of captured time in that empty room alone
Two figures from another age, their lives to me unknown.
But I saw the fate of a ragged child in the chimney's awful gloom
While a cruel master urged him on to a dark and awful doom.

There was nothing else but a fireplace in that vast and empty room.
As dark as death and as deep as time and as sure as the Fates own
loom
I fled the sights and I fled the sounds but the terror holds me tight
And I know I'll live it all again when I close my eyes tonight.

Catbird

There once was a cat that climbed a tree
and wouldn't come down at all.
He built a nest in a sheltered spot

118

and said he'd never fall.
Well he never fell, but his fur wore off
and feathers bloomed instead.
He grew two wings where his front legs were
and a beak upon his head.
He learned to sing as the sun came up
and slept when the red sun fell.
He even tried to lay an egg
and he managed very well.
The catbird sat upon his egg
to keep it warm and dry.
But nothing hatched from the catbird's egg
and nobody knows why.

Mark Tomlinson is a 49 year old father of four from Formby. He dabbles in poems and short stories and some people like them. He isn't one of those people so that's why he keeps trying.

The Complete Sign Service

361 Stockton Road
Hartlepool
TS25 1JX

Tel: (01429) 277250 • Fax: (01429) 235668

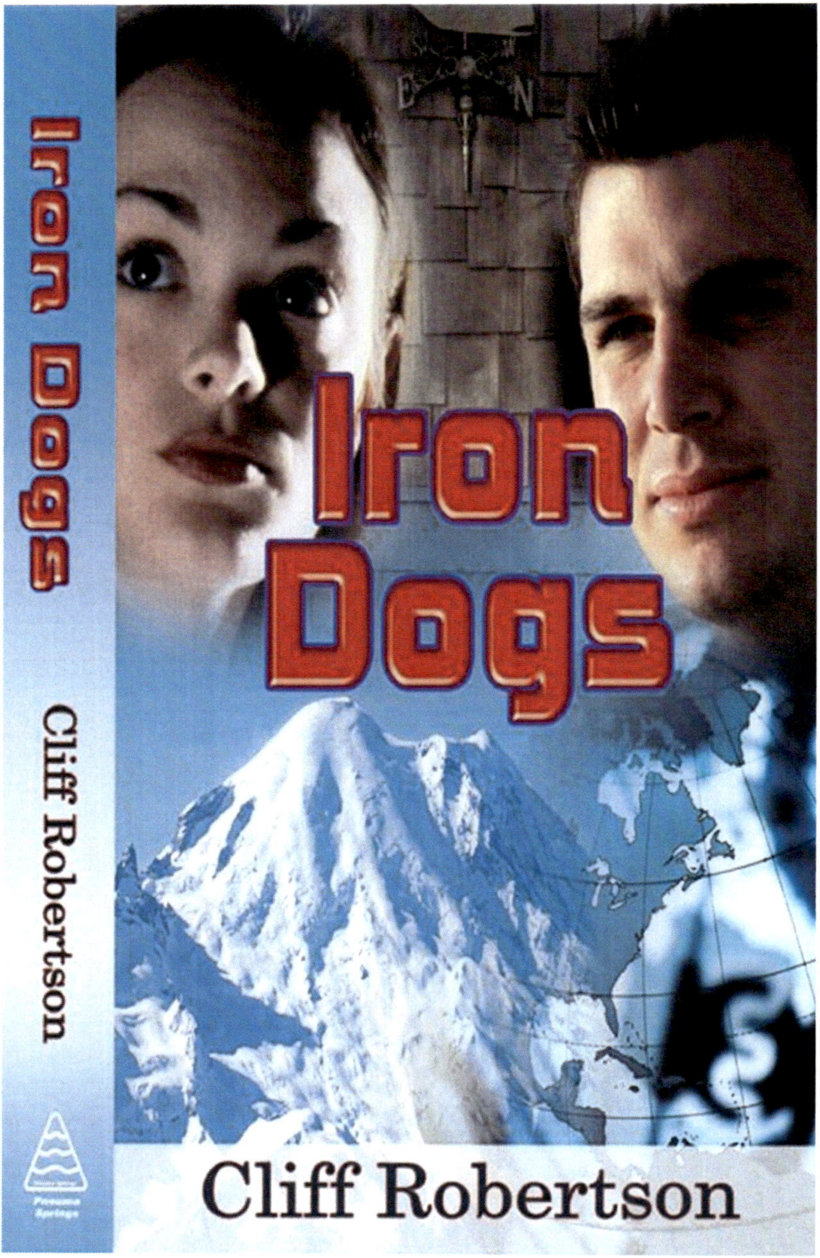
Iron Dogs
Cliff Robertson
Iron Dogs
Cliff Robertson

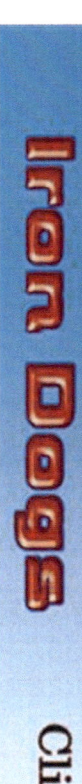

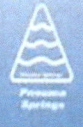

Chapter 26 .. Gary Hewitt

Modern love

Is his dick worth the fare? Dunno to be honest. I sit at my screen thinking about the day he first bothered my inbox. Three fateful yet simple words, well, actually one was a letter but let's not be fussy eh?

'U look hot,'

As a rule, I'd have fucked him off to the recycle bin but one look at the Lovebungler's picture hooked me. A click later and I was windows shopping on his profile. He had his top off and a carved six pack stared back at me. Yeah, he was buff alright.

He was interested in women, clubbing, women, football, women. He's about deep as a puddle of piss but so what. I'm fucked off with these sad pricks who go on about how they sit indoors reading or having saddo hobbies like growing frigging cactuses or cacti or whatever the fuck it is. I mean, some nutjob from Fulham seemed a bit decent. Well, until I finally took his virtual hand and went up West for a date. Did he kiss me? Did he give me a hug and go for some love? Did he bollocks. All frigging night he started going on about these bloody succulents and plants he had got in from Mexico, Bolivia or somewhere like that in America. I've never been so fucking bored in all my twenty two years. What was his name again? Oh yeah, Stewart James or the Thorny One to his online muckers. Should have guessed he'd be a wanker. Still, he's old news and now I'm looking at me latest e-mail from the Lovebungler.

'Babes, Y don't you get a train down here for Friday? It's only sixty eight quid and I'll show you the sights. Laterz if U R good I'll let I U play wiv my Robin Hood.'

Nottingham's a bloody long way away from Clapham though. I punch up a picture of him. A personal one. I've gotta say, he's Robin Hood is more than good and I wouldn't mind shoving it inside. He promised me at least five hours of fun in his dungeon. I come back that question again. Is his dick worth sixty eight sovs though and shouldn't he be forking out the cash?

My mind is set.

Very nice but I don't think so.

Fuck it, I think I'll go out with Aisha and Sharon instead and look for some local talent.

In the Lap of The Gods. (4TG)

Corston stood alone and espied the enemy. The trespasser took several steps forward. A bellicose warcry from his left invaded his secrecy. Corston threw himself into the orange undergrowth terrified. A trembling hand slipped to the side of a blood axe. He could not understand the hostile curses and threats.

'Harere kujjliglna setirioep Bassion?'

The enemy picked up his spoor and drew closer.

Corston prayed. He asked the seven Gods of Aparthia to give succour. He felt the ground darken in shadow and pulled himself upright roaring in defiance.

The Sammagian soldiers blinked astonished. They had expected an easy kill. Not a raging Bassion ravager eager for death.

They fled.

Corston growled at their cowardice. The God's were on his side. He felt himself beginning to rise, to fly on the wings of divinity.

'Got one.'

'Good.'

'What shall we do with the specimen?'

The Captain wanted at least one example alive.

'Take it to the examination hold. What manner of creature is it?'

'Biped. It has limited intellectual capacity although they have the ability to communicate at a simplistic level.'

'Will we be able to converse?'

'Undoubtedly. It probably thinks we're some kind of deity.'

Laughter followed. For the merest moment the Captain felt a pang of sympathy.

'The creature's now onboard.'

The officer led an entourage into the laboratory to find the creature being undressed. It stared in mute incomprehension when it's four arms were tethered to the examination slab. The creature's solitary ear was invaded by a probe of silver. Grey uniformed scientists employed mandible restraints and began to work.

'Captain, we have convinced the beast we are one of the seven Gods of Aparthia. He calls himself Corston of the Bassion tribe. I think Bassion seems an apt name don't you?' asked the chief Genetech officer.

The Captain agreed.

'What about any other organisms in the vicinity?'

'We caught one Sir. Unfortunately it suffered cardiac seizure. Shame, it was a good specimen.'

'Well catch another.'

The Scientist pointed at his display.

'Unfortunately, those other creatures wouldn't survive the trauma of space travel. Unlike the Bassion animal, they possess a very low tolerance to extreme stress.'

The Captain glanced at the dead humanoid animal.

'What will you do with it?'

The scientist pointed to a large machine adorned with sharp metal. 'We will eviscerate the specimen and store the remains for later evaluation.'

A cry shook the Captain from his relaxed mood. Several grey forms rushed towards the captured Bassion. The Captain followed the Genetech officer who took command of the panicking scientists.

'Are you the Gods? Why are you treating me so bad?'

'Yes we are. Relax, we are merely testing your strength mighty warrior.'

Corston struggled.

'Less of that, calm down.' The Genetech's voice strained in impatience.

'What about my family? Where are you taking me?'

The Captain offered a smile and stroked the animal's pitted brow.

'We'll come for your kin later. We're taking you to paradise. It's a place we call Earth.'

Gary Hewitt is forty years old and has been writing for a few years treating it as a hobby. He gets a thrill out of creating a story and he's well advanced into the first draft of his debut novel. Several of his stories have been included in anthologies from the Write Idea, Slingink and the Grail's writeathon in 2007. His stories try to be original, with writing that tends to be very much on the dark side! He lives in a small village near Kent and works in London, but his ultimate aim is to be a full time writer.

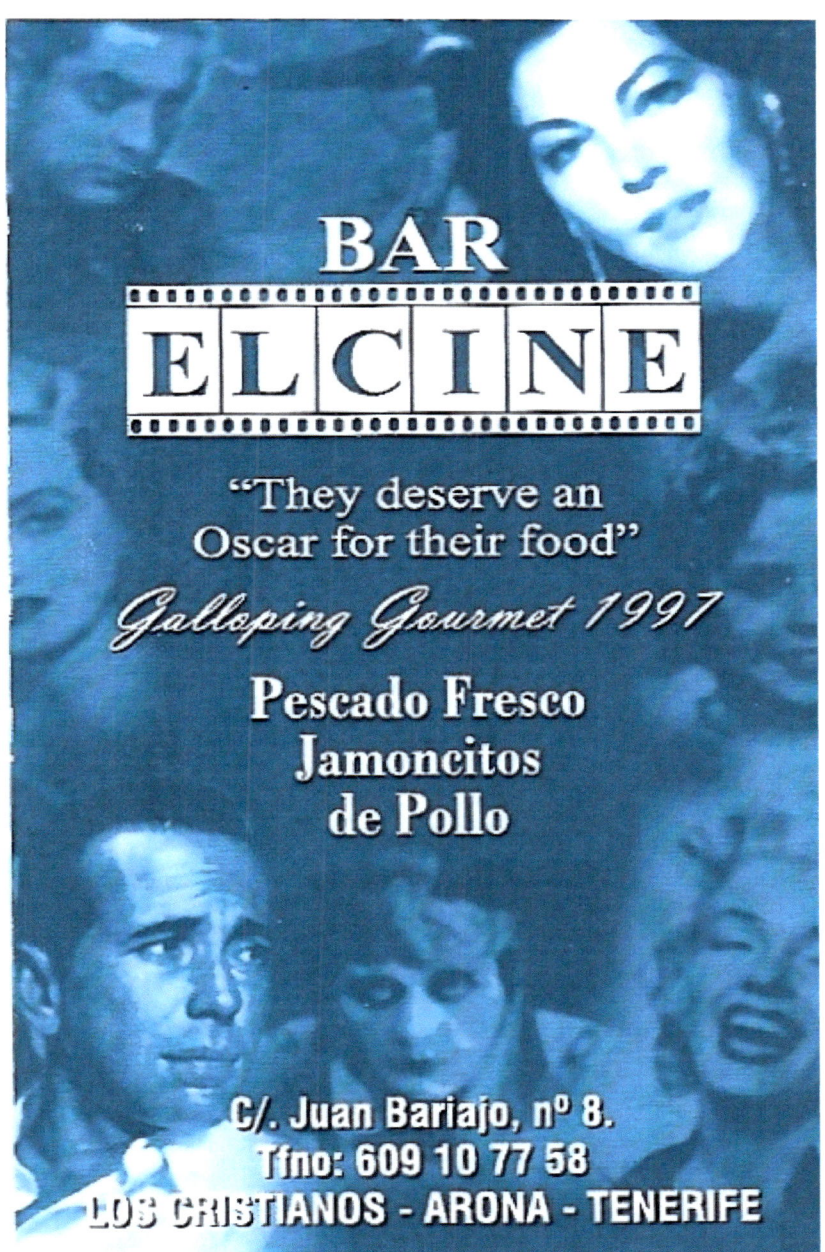

Cormorant
Publishing
East Anglia

Susan Ainslie
Tel: 01473 829917
Mob: 07522078832
47 Oxford Drive, Hadleigh, Ipswich IP7 6AW
Cormorant Publishing Ltd t/a Cormorant Publishing East Anglia

THE GOLD MEDAL WINNER FOR A WARM WELCOME

Brendan and Annette will ensure that while you will arrive a stranger you will leave a friend.

The Devon Arms. Calle Juan XIII, Los Cristianos.
Tel: 922 753 647